HOOKED ON A 5TH

WARD MENACE 2

BY MS. GRAD MARIE

About the Author

Authoress Ms. Grad Marie

"Even though characters are fictional, I believe we all have a story to tell."

National best-selling Authoress Ms. Grad Marie is a Texas native. She writes in a young adults point of view. Ms. Grad Marie published her first urban fiction novel in the fall of 2017: titled Share my World with a Savage Like You.

She now has Eleven titles under her belt with more to come. Ms. Grad Marie began writing at the tender age of only twelve years old. Writing helped her escape from her harsh reality.

Ms. Grad Marie's word of advice to new and upcoming authors is: "if it's on your mind...write it off! Pick up the pen and write your way out." "and to never, ever, doubt yourself."

She enjoys being the mother of two spoiled brats lol

Cooking, decorating, and divatizing

msgradmarie@gmail.com

To My Lovies

Thank you thank you thank you! You guys have been riding tough witcha girl since I started posting short stories on my page in 2016.

I want to thank each and every one of you that support me both near and far!

If you would've asked me three years ago if I've ever thought about being a published author I wouldn't know exactly what my answer would be but look at me now!

I thank all of my Book Lovaz for being patient, caring, honest and there for me not only with my books!

I thank you all for loving Grad just for who she is! Again, thanks for your continued support my loves 💋

SYNOPSIS

Monika did the unthinkable to her own flesh and blood. She's been holding in so many secrets and lies about herself and the man she's madly in love with. Will she turn on J-Don to free herself from the agonizing pain of their past? Or will everything she's tried to sweep under the rug come back and reveal itself?

Sometimes lessons not learned in blood are easily forgotten and you have to remind people just who they're interfering with...

Where we left off

Malik

I checked myself in the floor length mirror again, making sure I was straight before snatching my keys and phone off the dresser. I was glad that MiKi had finally agreed to go out with a nigga after me trying so hard. I had a special night planned for us with the help of my homegirl, Myia. Most females weren't into sports and shit but seeing the way Miki shot that three pointer the night we took the kids out for dinner let me know that she was a versatile chick. Her son, Xavion, had game too. I hooked him up with my homeboy who owned a youth rec center and a basketball team.

I darted down the hallway to the elevator and rode it to the parking garage. I had reserved us a section at the Rockets game tonight and afterwards, if she was up for it, I scheduled us his and her massages in a luxurious sky suite at the Mosaic Towers downtown. I gave Myia some bread earlier, so she could make the place look nice by adding some rose petals, champagne and all that other girly shit chicks liked.

I know that I had never been in a committed relationship before, but Miki made me long for one. It was something about her that made a nigga wana do right and stop fucking random bitches every now and then. We still hadn't been together sexually since the first night we met. I wasn't going to pressure her into the bed. I was more than willing to wait until she was ready. She kept me intrigued during our hour long daily conversations. She knew I was a street nigga and never judged me. Plus, every time I woke up in the morning, I grinned like a lil kid reading how she texted me good morning and to be safe in the streets.

I made it to the parking garage at my crib and popped the locks on my drop top to show off a bit. Forty-five minutes later, I pulled up to the Manor ready to see my date. My dick hardened in my jeans watching the way Miki sashayed her thick ass down the sidewalk, rocking a deep purple maxi dress, painting her curvaceous body that I couldn't wait to wrap in my arms. Grabbing the medium bouquet of mixed, bright colored flowers from the passenger seat, I jigged out my mustang at a fast pace to meet shorty halfway.

"Damn, Mami. You rockin' the hell out that fit," I flirted with her, biting my bottom lip and showcasing my blinged out bottom grill as I pulled her deep into my embrace.

"Thanks, Malik. You're looking mighty swell yourself!" She flirted back with me, brushing her soft hands down my shirt. I wrapped my arm around her waist right above that fat ass booty she lugged around and walked her down the sidewalk.

"Hey, Malik! Have fun, Mama, and bring me something back!" Xavion shouted from the window of Ms. Jackie's apartment.

"Boy, get yo' butt in that bed!" She giggled embarrassingly back at her son.

I walked her to the passenger side and held open the door for her. When she was seated comfortably, I jogged around to the driver's side and slid in.

"Thanks for the flowers, babe. They're beautiful." She beamed at me, reaching for my free hand to intertwine our fingers.

"You're welcome. Thanks for finally giving me some play and allowing me to take you out. Hold on for a minute, boo." I pecked her hands and flicked my tongue across it before letting her go and scrolling my phone. Seeing the way Miki was dressed tonight, I couldn't let her bust a sweat in that dress with all the walking we would do at a basketball game, so I hit up my homie Black to see if he could make us last minute reservations at a fancy restaurant.

"What up, bro? Damn, aww, for real? Ok, cool. I'll see if I can come up with something. Bet."

"Is something wrong?" My caramel beauty asked with worried eyes.

"Nah, boo, nothing is wrong. I—I just had plans for us to see the Rockets play tonight. But seeing how you came downstairs looking like America's next top model and shit, I figure maybe we could just have dinner or something before our scheduled massages."

I swallowed the lump in my throat and waited on her response. I exhaled in frustration, hoping that I didn't ruin our lil date night. I wanted tonight to be a total surprise, so I didn't give her a heads up on where we were going. I just told her to rock something sexy. Shit, she could've came out in a fucking trash bag and still would've been the most beautiful woman in the world to me next to my mama.

"Do we need to swing back to the house, so I can change? I'm sorry, I should've asked for an idea of where we were going." She put her head down.

"No, baby. I don't want you taking that dress off, unless you want me taking it off." I grabbed her hand again, locking her fingers with mines. "I had his and her massages planned for us after the game at my suite downtown. Do you just wana go there now and order in dinner?"

My chest waved waiting on her response. I didn't want Mami thinking a nigga was just tryna get in her drawers. I mean, I wouldn't ever forget that good ass pussy I still dreamed about, but it was no pressure. Shit, I had just did three years fucking nothing but Palmesha, so I was straight on fucking something for a bit. I'd rather get money 'til the right woman came my way, and she was all mine.

"Sure, Leek, that's fine. I'm all yours for tonight. So, whatever you have planned is fine with me." She sat back in the seat so relaxed as I gripped the wheel with my left hand like the incredible Hulk to control my rising dick.

She said she was all mines tonight. Hopefully soon, I could change that into forever. I don't know what it was about Miki, but I craved her. I wanted her and wanted to be only hers forever.

Monika

Estaban thought that me fucking him was so I could own my clothing boutique, but in truth, I was saving up for the day I was preparing to leave J-Don's ass. I grew tired of his shit. And by Malik getting arrested awhile back, it put a damper in our household's pockets. I had been hiding notices from the bank and bill collectors, but we were not doing good as we put on. Shit, we were down bad and it's all because of his greedy ass baby mama.

J-Don's dumb ass was scared of that stupid bitch, and she had him by the balls. To avoid Caresha placing a court order monthly child support fee in his life, his bitch ass paid all that hoe's bills monthly. We stayed getting into it behind that hoe. He claimed I didn't understand and shit was different because he was a man. Caresha took advantage of his kindness and held those kids ransom, using them poor babies to her advantage. My nigga was too stupid to see that shit though, so I stopped talking about it.

Who was I to tell that nigga about baby mama, baby daddy drama anyway? Atmos didn't give a fuck about me or T'Asia. I got tired of watching him and his bug-eyed fiancé monkey shinning on the book daily like they were so happy. Everybody knew that nigga was beating her ass then going to the MAC store in the mall buying all the Rhianna Fenty out so that ugly hoe could cover up her scars. I would NEVER trust any of these hoes that put on for social media when I know the absolute truth about them. Can't no bitch make me mad about a nigga I done had, or a nigga I'm still fucking.

I arrived at the ground floor, walking over to the valet booth, so they could get my car. I halted when my name was called behind me. Chills instantly covered my body as the familiar voice continued to call me. I pretended to ignore him and walked at a fast pace through the double automatic doors, only stopping when he yanked my arm.

"Monika Smith. I have been trying to reach you lately, but you've been ignoring my calls. Guess we have to chat in person now, huh?" Detective Martinez evilly smiled, gritting his coffee stained teeth. I crossed my arms, avoiding his eyes that grazed my body then stopped when they connected with my eyes.

"You've been with him again, huh?" He demanded me to answer him, already knowing the truth behind his question. "I can smell it. You reek of expensive Cuban cigars and old man cum!" He shouted, making me jump and alerting a couple that was passing by to check-in.

"I just came here for a business meeting, nothing personal," I lied through my teeth, hoping that he would loosen his jaws of life grip he held on my body.

"I'm tired of you doing this shit to me. You don't know what the fuck you want. You're sleeping with the fucking enemy. You promised me you were done, yet I find your ass over here again, sneaking out like Michael Jackson with a silk scarf wrapped around your head. I've given you too many chances to make shit right between us. I'm giving you three weeks to give me what I'm owed or you and your little family business will come tumbling down, do you understand me?" He barked, sending more fear through my trembling body.

"I got you, nigga, ok? Three weeks, I got it. Now let me the fuck go," I pleaded, trying to hide my face from the continuous stares of people steady coming in and out of the building.

He finally granted my request, letting me go as valet returned with my ride. I knew this day would come sooner or later and I had to woman up and not punk out. I never thought shit would be like this, but this is the life you sign up for when you commit to a known street nigga.

***

I sprung up from my deep slumber that was induced by the several shots of tequila I downed earlier. Looking at the time on my cell that read 1:40 am, I felt a rush of Deja vu covering me again. Standing to walk to our adjacent bathroom to release my full bladder, I avoided my reflection in the large mirror. I felt like a fucking idiot, so I'm pretty sure I looked like one too. Toying with the string on my bright red lace teddy, I tried to fill my head with positive thoughts.

You're tripping, Nika, stop tripping. Maybe he got caught up in some business. He said he had to go talk to Malik, so maybe they were out handling some shit and he will come home covered in blood, begging me to strip the evidence as usual.

I finished my business, wiped and flushed, then lathered up my hands and washed them. An eerie feeling filled my brain as I dried my hands. Today of all days, this nigga couldn't keep his promise and come home on time. It was our fucking anniversary and here I was, dressed up, face beat to the Gawds with a fresh sew in from Miki, waiting on my nigga.

I pulled up the tracker app on my phone. I felt that I hadn't had a reason to check it lately because J-Don was acting right. Since our last fight, that nigga had been courting me like the queen my mother birthed me to be. A couple months ago, I stashed a tracker on his truck. J had a couple cars, but his truck is the one he used the most when he wanted to be incognegro. I clicked the app and waited uneasily with anticipation as it loaded. My palms dripped with perspiration as my heart beat like a bass drum screaming to escape my exposed chest. Not even a minute later, the location of my lying, cheating ass nigga popped up on my screen.

I sprinted back to the bathroom sick to my stomach. I couldn't believe this hoe ass nigga. Searching through my make-up caboodle, I was satisfied when I found what I was looking for, my eyebrow razor. Darting back to the bedroom, I began to stab the heart shape balloons, piercing them to release the payment my heart felt as tears streamed from my eyes. Fuck this shit. I was too good of a bitch to him and his hoe ass family. Lying for them and keeping their secrets for years. It was time for that nigga to pay for all the pain I caused. Jaidion wasn't shit like he portrayed to be out there in those streets. He was a snitch that betrayed every single nigga's path he crossed, even his own brother and father.

I laughed evilly, glancing at the now popped and deflated balloons, glitter and rose petals that covered our bed and floor. It was time to let all this nigga's skeletons out the closet. Jumping up to my feet, I skipped to the closet in search of something to throw on. After getting dressed, I picked up my phone again, deciding to make sure my eyes weren't playing tricks on me. I knew Caresha's address by heart, and I know that broke bitch didn't move, or maybe she did because the address showed me somewhere in third ward.

Filled with even more fury, I snatched my purse off the dresser, grabbed my keys and headed to the garage. Hopping in my whip, I impatiently waited for the garage to raise before backing out, screeching my tires like a mad woman. I hit the trashcan on the way out and knocked some things off a shelf, but I didn't give a fuck, I was on a mission. Throwing my gear shift in drive, I was headed to the freeway doing 80 in a 60. I scrolled through my news feed on the book the whole way there, making sure I deleted all the post I made earlier about my perfect relationship I monkey shined for. I had over 400 likes and comments on the pictures I'd posted earlier of our decked out bedroom. I couldn't do anything but shake my head. I was really dumb as fuck behind this community dick ass nigga.

Forty-minutes later, I crept down the street my phone led me to and low and behold, there sat Jaidion's truck, backed up on the driveway like that nigga lived there.

"I know this bitch ass, lil dick muh fucka is not over here with some bitch playing house!" I screamed out loud, hoping that by me hearing my own words I could believe them.

Tapping my thumbs on my steering wheel, I tried to calm my rising blood pressure down to a minimum. I wanted to cry like a bitch, but the greater part of me wanted to run up on his bitch ass. Without hesitation, I jigged out my ride and rushed from across the street where I was parked. Not giving a hot damn if I woke the neighborhood, I banged my heavy fists on the clear screen door until someone flicked on the porch light. The front door swung open and there stood a preteen with wide, doe-shaped eyes. Baby girl was a beautiful, dark skinned little girl who looked just like Jaidion. I became short-winded and lost my balance as I ran away from the porch and back across the street. I hopped in the driver's seat, cranked my engine and obeyed all traffic signals on the way home.

I felt defeated and betrayed, but most of all, vengeful. There's only one way I could always make sure of that nigga's whereabouts. I wouldn't have to worry about him touching any bitch or being backed up on their driveway's playing house. It was time for J-Don to sit down for a minute. Killing him would be too easy. He needed to pay for every fucked up thing he did out here in these streets and what he did to me.

Exiting off the freeway, I dialed up Detective Martinez's number. Since the day I saw him leaving Estaban's, he had been calling me daily to remind me that he would lock my ass up if I didn't give him what he wanted. All pigs were dirty ass fuck if you asked me. Martinez needed the Davis boys out of business because them working under Estaban put the Martinez boys under fire, and they hated competition. Those laws weren't stupid. They knew that behind every Dope boy was his secret keeping bitch. Shit, even El Chapo's wife knew what the fuck was going on, she just didn't speak on it.

I pulled into our driveway and killed my lights, waiting for him to answer. Jumping out the driver's seat and sprinting up the small stairs that led to the red brick porch, I ran inside to my bedroom beaming.

"Ahh yes, Nika. Speak, whatcha got for me, love?" He inquired, making me hear the way his teeth cracked while smiling.

"I got something for you. Can you meet me in about 30 mins?"

"Sure, love. Just give me the location."

We decided to meet each other close to downtown, not too far from where I just left. I had to make sure J-Don's newfound daughter didn't go back and report to her parents that she'd seen me at the door of their home, and he was out looking for me. Being that he hadn't hit my line since I left third ward, I felt that maybe baby girl hadn't alerted them of some strange woman banging on the door late at night. Or two, he could've known it was me and decided to just not say anything. Either way, I knew he wouldn't make it home tonight. The only place he was going was to county jail.

Pulling open the door to my large walk-in closet, I hit the light and started digging through boxes. I couldn't remember exactly where I stashed it, but I knew it was here where it had been since four years ago when I pried it from J-Don's hands the night he wanted to kill himself. I wanted to break it down and toss it like he trained and requested me to do every weapon him and his family used to end a nigga's life, but I decided to keep it for insurance. See, if that nigga would've did right by me, I wouldn't be doing this fuck shit, but he just couldn't seem to keep his lil burnt vienna sausage in his designer jeans that I paid for.

I walked out my closet wanting to give up, then remembered that I had hidden what I was looking for in the garage. Running through the house like an excited kid on Christmas, I barged into the garage feeling successful of my accomplishment. Walking over to the shelf above the washer and dryer, I stretched on my tip-toes, reaching for the black tool box that held so many secrets and so much evidence of open cold cases. I pulled the box down filled with adrenaline, preparing myself to open it up when something that was stuck in the garage door caught my eye. Sitting the box down, I slowly walked with heavy feet towards the body that was lying sprawled out on the cold, concrete floor.

"T. T'Asia?!" I called for my decaying daughter who laid unresponsive. Quickly, I pulled her limp body back into the garage then ran to the other side in search of the closing button.

"Oh, my fucking goodness! I-I killed my fucking daughter?!" I said in a low tone, not to alert the neighborhood.

Secretly thanking the man upstairs that no one had found her yet, I thought quickly about what I needed to do. When I zoomed out the garage earlier to go find my cheating ass nigga, I thought I had bumped into the trash can. I'd forgotten that my mother dropped T'Asia back home earlier. Shit, she was with my mother so much, motherhood wasn't something I claimed unless it was time to get some benefits for her. I know it was a fucked up situation, but it was kind of a blessing in disguise because this was one less thing I had to deal with.

I pulled several extra-large trash bags from a drawer, placed them on the floor, then walked over to grab my daughter. I've done this so many times before that I knew how to dispose of a dead fish. I lifted her decaying body from the floor, placed it on the plastic and rolled her ass like an old, worn out carpet. I grabbed a nearby pair of leather gloves and duct tape to bind her hands and feet. When I was satisfied with her security, I ran through the house, grabbing a set of Jdon's keys and pulled his car into the garage.

"Fuck, bitch! You're really getting a work out tonight." I laughed to myself before lifting my daughter's remains into the trunk of the Camaro.

I grabbed a bottle of bleach to clean the blood stains from the door and floor. I had to work fast because of where we lived, it was always an old, white, nosey motherfucker neighborhood watching everybody's business on the block. I sat the bleach in the trunk along with the toolbox before reopening the garage and backing onto the driveway. I felt like a mad woman and if someone was watching me, I'm sure they could figure out something wasn't right. I pulled my car into the garage finally, making sure it was clear of evidence. The impact hurt my daughter, but my real baby, my Benz truck was safe and sound.

Remembering that I had an appointment to keep to frame my sorry ass nigga, I jumped in the driver's seat of his Camaro and hit the freeway with Glee. I don't know why this nigga tried me, he knew I was a crazy bitch!

J-Don

"Who was that at the door?" Keke walked up behind me as I watched Monika's truck speed off the street.

"I don't know, baby. Probably someone who had the wrong house," I lied, praying that she couldn't read my body language I tried to hide.

"Baby girl answered the door half sleep, but I sent her back to bed." I closed the door, securing it before I lifted Keara up, straddling her legs around my waist.

She wrapped her smooth, chocolate hands that felt like silk around the back of my neck then started sucking on the side of my neck, making my soldier stand up at attention again for the fourth time tonight.

"Let's go back to bed, baby," she cooed in my arms as we made our way back to the bedroom.

We reached the bedroom to finish our sex session, and I closed the door quickly with my foot, not letting go of the woman I've always truly loved and wanted to be with. With Monika, I had to be a hood nigga because that was what she was accustomed to. But with Keke, I could be the real me, Jaidion.

I provided for her and my kids and put her through school twice to better herself. Being a nigga in the streets, tomorrow was never promised, so I wanted to make sure mine were taking care of. I knew her twins weren't mine because after me fucking over on her and playing with her heart with these sack chasing hoes out here, she showed me a reality check by fucking with another nigga. She said the only reason she kept the twins is because they had a chance of being mine.

I sat her down gently on the bed and slowly unwrapped the silk robe that covered her gorgeous body.

"Damn, nigga. You ain't gon' let me rest, huh?" She laughed, laying back on the soft bed as I spread her legs open. "Stop it, Jaidion Davon Davis! She's sore, let her rest a little bit," she begged as I ignored her. I wrapped my large lips around her pearl tongue that poked out under the hood of her juicy pussy peeking at me.

I didn't give a fuck about anything else in the world right now. I had promised Keke that we would no longer have to sneak fuck in one of the empty apartments at Cleme manor anymore. I was ready to be with the woman I loved at all costs. She loved me flaws and all and my children. We needed to be under one roof as a family.

Miki

As I walked around my apartment straightening up and getting ready for my next client, I smiled, reminiscing on my date last week with Malik. At first, I was surprised that we were actually laying butt naked in front of each other and didn't fuck each other's brains out. I knew he wanted me as much as I wanted him, but I didn't want another fuck buddy. I would be thirty soon and I felt as if I was too old for that. We ordered dinner from some expensive steak house he recommended, and the massages were much needed, relaxing and wonderful, especially when Malik took over and helped my massage guy out. He was a gentle thug. The way his strong, but soft hands caressed my body had my pussy dripping all over them people table. He got me to open up a bit about my background and family, but I would never give anyone the complete truth about me. I left that shit back in Galveston county.

I ran to the counter to pick up my ringing phone hoping that it was Malik since I couldn't get him off my brain. For the past couple weeks, we had been doing a date night weekly, so I couldn't wait to see what he had planned this weekend. When I finally got to my phone, the caller hung up. Seeing that the number wasn't saved, I decided to wait until they called back. Many people hit my line up daily for quotes and prices on my infamous hair styles. I figured if they really wanted to talk to me about business then they could call again.

Checking the time on my cell, I saw that it was close to three. I had an appointment scheduled for 2:30, but I saw they were running late. Maybe that was the person that just called and hung up. I clicked on the number, scrolled through the message thread in my phone and saw that the number wasn't from the client I was expecting today.

Shrugging my shoulders and walking to the kitchen to see what I could defrost for dinner, I heard someone tap on my screen door. I looked over at the woman standing outside the door who seemed familiar. Goosebumps veiled my body as I stepped closer to the door viewing her face. It had been several years since I'd seen Kitty. She looked like she had taken a trip or two to Dr. Miami or the Dominican

Republic, but it was her. I knew this day would come, I just didn't know when. But it was here, and I couldn't run from shit that was brought to my doorstep. Exhaling through my nose, I bit my bottom lip and unlatched the screen door.

"Well, hello to you too, Miki," she greeted me in an unpleasant tone. "Why do you look shocked and scared? You weren't scared when I gave you a place to stay when your mama put yo' ass out in the streets, huh? And how do you repay me? Someone you called your sister and friend, forever 'til the end. You not only fucked my husband, Xavier, nightly under my roof and in our bed, but you got pregnant by the nigga and had his fucking son! Then you tried to escape Galveston county like your dirty little secrets weren't going to follow your trifling ass," she sneered, filling my body with rage.

Cotton mouth instantly stopped my words, and I was stuck were I stood. What brought me out of the devilish trance I was in is when Xavion came running through the screen door, the spitting image of my ex-best friend's husband, Xavier.

Meeting Xavier

Xavier was fine as fuck!

He was only about 5'10", but he had this medium build that was chiseled being that he was a star on the varsity football team. His muscles looked strong enough to knock a nigga out. He had a dark caramel complexion with the biggest, prettiest lips that I'd ever seen on a man. He stayed fly as hell, always dressed in the latest and most popular designer labels. Even his teeth were perfectly white, and his soft, brown eyes had the nerve to sparkle when he smiled, revealing deep, crater-like dimples. He was perfect.

We were freshman, and he was a junior. The older I got, the more I fantasized about him being my first, falling in love with me, and leaving those ratchet hood rats that flocked behind him on a daily alone.

One day I was walking home from after school detention for getting caught in the boys' locker room, and Xavier drove by in his hooptie smiling at me. I waved to his fine ass, accidentally distracting him, making him temporarily take his eyes off the road and causing him to swerve to avoid hitting a minivan. I tried to hide my laughter when I saw him pull into a nearby driveway to turn around. By the time I reached the next crossing part of the street, he was parked at the end waiting for me. A relieved look now washed over his face as he met me with a wide smile.

"Come here, Miki girl. You need a ride home?" He asked, making my brown cheeks flush a cherry red.

I only had about two more blocks to go, but I'd dreamt of this moment for the past couple of years, so I nodded my head and hopped in his passenger seat when he reached over and opened the door for me. About five minutes later, we were pulling up to my house.

"Thanks again for the, ride friend. I told you I didn't have that far to go, but I walk slow sometimes because I come home to an empty house until my mother gets off." I let him know.

"Well, I can sit with you for a few minutes if you'd like. Practice was cancelled today because coach was sick, so I don't have to be home for a couple hours." He stopped abruptly, first looking at the door of my house then back at me.

"That's cool. Just pull your car out the street, but don't park in my Mama's driveway please!" I reminded him, hopping out the passenger seat and swaying my hips fully in his view as he straightened his car. I was tired of being the only sexually curious girl in the ninth grade click without a boyfriend who's cherry hadn't been popped yet. Shit, even Kitty got some dick before I did.

Soon, he was lightly jogging behind me, eager for what I had in store for him. I walked to the kitchen to get us something to snack on and when I returned to the living room, Xavier was sitting on the couch with his ballers at his ankles and his massive piece in his hands stroking it. Little did he know, I was a virgin. Outside of playing with my pussy, I didn't know the first thing about fucking.

"Why you looking at it like that? You scared of this dick?" He flirtatiously asked, biting his bottom lip which trembled as he continued jacking himself off.

"No, I ain't scared of nothing, especially nothing I never had." I flirted back with him.

I took no time pulling off my cheerleader skirt and panties that had a puddle of my cream between them. I hopped on top of Xavier, wrapping my arms around his thick neck. His lips brushed my ear, raising goosebumps across my bare legs. Xavier rubbed his hands down my waist, grabbing the arc of my hips with his thumbs, pulling himself deeper into my untouched love box. I rolled my eyes to the back of my head, my mouth twisted in a pleasured smirk at the greatness I was receiving between my shaky legs. It felt uncomfortable at first, but a good hurt. Our bodies meshed together as we flowed in a gentle rhythm, pleasing each other. His nonstop panting alerted me that he was probably coming close to his climax. I felt my coochie warming up the more he thrust me, so I knew that I would be joining him shortly. Masturbating on a daily couldn't compare to the feeling Xavier was giving me at this moment. I screamed in satisfaction and a lone tear fell from my eye.

When I brought my head back to an upright position, my mother was standing there behind the couch, watching us with crossed arms. My breath caught in my throat, then I exhaled in a series of shorts breaths. My mother snatched me from on top of Xavier by my freshly braided hair and threw me to the floor like a rag doll. In between throws from Mommy Dearest's strong fists, I could hear my date's feet scuffling the floor, making his way to the door.

"You nasty bitch!" My mother yelled, continuing to bruise my body with her bare hands.

I laid unmoving and silent, praying that it would cause her to cease the abuse if she thought she killed me. I knew I shouldn't have been caught fucking in the living room of my mother's home, but if she would've told me about the birds and the bees when I asked numerous times before, I wouldn't have had the curiosity to find out what it felt like on my own.

She finally grew tired of fighting me and stopped. I laid in a fetal position a few more moments until she came and dragged me from where I was, stripped me naked and threw my limp body in the tub of running water. I squinted my eyes at her, watching her pour half a bottle of bleach on my body, attempting to wash away my dirty sins of losing my virginity.

By my mother acting as if sex was a forbidden sin, she just opened me up to wanting it more. This was only the first time I had snuck a boy into my mother's house without her knowing, but the more I did it, the more I knew not to get caught. After my mother's long work shifts the only thing she wanted was sleep, her TV, and her bottle of crown. As soon as I noticed that brown crown had her ass knocked the fuck out it was time for me to play.

The best things in life were things you weren't supposed to have, and Xavier was one of them.

Chapter One

Monika

Tears crept from my eyes as I rushed down the freeway. My current emotions were uncontrollable and unexplainable. I hated being a mother at times because I felt that I was forced to be one. The type of mother I had, she didn't care about me being a teenager who didn't know the first thing about motherhood. She felt that if I was grown enough to open my legs to Atmos then I was grown enough to push a baby out and take care of it. If I would've called anyone and told them that I just accidentally hit my daughter, every judge in the state of Texas would give me the fucking death sentence. I didn't want to be the one held responsible for her death, but I knew I had to get rid of her body ASAP!

My cell ringtone blaring snapped me out of my thoughts. I picked it up from the passenger seat to answer Martinez's call. I wasn't sure if I wanted to meet him now after finding my daughter.

"Damn it, T'Asia! Why the fuck yo' ass wasn't inside where I left you!" I screamed, letting out the pain I felt inside.

Up until I met J-Don, T'Asia was a non-verbal autistic child. Another reason why I loved him is because that nigga loved the shit out of his kids. Especially mine that his sperm didn't make.

What to do? What to fucking do Nika?! I debated with myself. I desperately wanted J-Don to pay for all the pain he caused me throughout the years and I realized that I needed his cheating ass now more than ever. I was going to have to report my daughter missing and put on a show for the cameras.

I ignored the Detective's call and shot him a quick text message.

Me: I-I can't find my daughter. She's missing! I'm sorry I can't meet you right at this moment. I need to find her.

Martinez called me once more and when he finally got the picture that I wasn't showing up tonight, he left me the fuck alone.

I had to think quick if I wanted to get away with this. I mashed the gas pedal, exiting off 45 and drove down the dark street until I reached a dead end that was near a deserted area by a pond. Making sure I wasn't being followed, I sat in my parked car for almost 15 minutes. Numbness covered my body. I had no emotions and no words to explain the events that were currently kicking my ass in life.

When the coast was clear, I backed up the car to the edge of the body of water I was familiar with many times before. I didn't appreciate my daughter, and I didn't deserve motherhood. Never in my thirty plus years of life would I ever think that this would be my only child's fate. It was best that I lost our son years ago because I didn't deserve him either.

I rubbed my weary eyes with the base of my palms, and put my emotions to the side as I hopped out the car and headed to the trunk. Pulling it open, I wasted no more time lifting my deceased daughter's remains from the trunk and tossing her deep into the water. A feeling of sadness shielded me as I watched her young body flow down the river. I headed back to the driver's side to hurry home, trying to gather my thoughts about what I would tell the police when I reported T'Asia missing. Then I spotted two crackheads emerging from behind the bushes just a few feet away from where I was parked. Before I could reach the door handle of my ride, a familiar voice called out my name.

"Nika! What you doin' back here, girl?" Lashay snickered, pulling her shorts from her ankles to her exposed hips. I noticed that she was with Buggy who was another known feen from my man's hood.

"What?" I arched a questioning eyebrow in her direction. I didn't have time for her pill begging ass today and deep inside, I wondered just how long they had been out there in the park.

By her face, I could tell a question kept gnawing at her. "You heard me girl! What you back here stashing in that water?" She cracked up laughing, and I could tell her ass was high as fuck.

Buggy stood in his own world, continuing to light the little glass dick he cupped in his dirty, ashy hands, dancing to a musical tune only feens could hear when they were full of that good dope. My face remained stuck, my eyes widened, and my amazement was hidden by a slow breath. Now I was going to have to murk this dope head hoe too. I hopped in my ride and sped off from her powder head ass with the quickness before she started begging me for dope.

Chapter Two

MiKisha

I stood caught like a deer in headlights.

"Go ahead and put your bookbag up, then you can go outside, Xai," I ordered to my son. I'm sure he could tell by my body language that I was tensed up. I wasn't discussing the truth about his existence and my past in front of him. He did as he was told, placed his things in his room and ran back outside with his friends.

"Now that my son is out of the room, let me tell you something, Kitty! One thing you're not going to do is come to my home uninvited and disrespect me in my shit. Number one!" I barked at her as she stood just a few feet away from me with folded arms, laughing.

"It's cool. I should've known that your lil hot in the twat ass wasn't a true friend and could never be trusted. Ray Charles can see that, that baby just might be my husband's, but you know what the old folks say. *A bitch could want a baby by a nigga so bad, that it could just come out looking like him.*" She cracked up laughing then pulled an envelope from her back pocket.

"If your little boy is my husband's then we will petition the court for full. By your living conditions and lil kitchen beautician business, we *will* win! See you in court, MiKisha." Kitty turned on her heels, darted towards the door and disappeared down the stairs just as quickly as she came.

I guess this bitch was the appointment I was waiting for. I thought to myself, walking over to the kitchen counter to retrieve the envelope she left behind. Opening the envelope, a rush of fear came over me. I was being served by Kitty and Xavier to determine the paternity of my son.

I kinda felt like that bitch Kitty just came in my house and punked the shit outta me. If circumstances were different and my son wouldn't have walked in, I probably would've slid that hoe across my project tile floor. How dare that hoe set up a fake hair appointment to come serve me some papers? She was really mad with the wrong person. Xavier is the one that stepped out on their "oh so perfect relationship". Plus, I met the nigga first. The life that he provider for her was supposed to be mines.

Summer 2010

"You expected me to give up my life for you, but you're grown now, honey! It's time for you to spread your wings and get the fuck from under my roof!" My mother yelled at me, pushing my back as she followed me around, making sure I gathered my small belongings.

I didn't know where I was going to go or what I was going to do, but I'd had enough of her bullying and bitching. My whole life I catered to her complaining ass, being her slave and making sure her house was spic and span. And all she did was abandoned me, locking me up like I was Cinderella my whole life.

"That's right, bitch, get your shit and get the fuck out! You ain't gonna be good enough for anything but to lay on your fucking back!"

When she screamed those last words at me, I completely lost it. I dropped the box I was carrying in my arms, turned on my heels and started wind-milling her ass like she was a bitch in the street. At this moment, I didn't give one fuck about her being the woman who birthed me. She had gone too far and that was real disrespectful.

Furious and with all her strength, she tried to push me off her, knocking me against the dining room table, shattering it in a million pieces. This didn't stop me. I lunged forward to meet her, jabbing my fists into her oversized stomach, hoping that she would get short winded and surrender. We went round for round, tag teaming each other until Kitty, who I texted earlier before this show started, showed up just in time to step in and stop my mother and I from killing each other.

"Kitty, get her! Get this bitch the fuck out of my got damn house! I don't want to ever see you again!" My mother hissed, venom dripping from her dry ass lips.

I granted her wish and did as I was told, never looking back at the home I grew up in alone, unattended to and unloved.

Two Weeks Later

I peeped the clock on the microwave that read 2:15. I had my headphones in and was jamming to Beyoncé's Bday album on my phone as I danced around the kitchen finishing up dinner and tidying up before Kitty came home from work. In about 30 minutes, I was scheduled to get her two kids off the bus, feed them diner and start their homework lessons.

I was so grateful for my friend that she gave me a place to stay after all that shit went down with my mama. I had a few clients whose hair I braided during the morning, then the afternoon I spent making sure Kitty and her kids came home to a clean house and a hot meal. If I couldn't do anything else, I could cook and clean. That's all I knew how to do and hair. I made the house extra comfortable for my friend and her kids so when she came home, she didn't have to worry about anything. She could just eat, bathe, and rest. I had to pay my way somehow being that I had no job, no ride and only a high school diploma.

Kitty: Hey boo. Xavier 'posed to be dropping by in a bit to bring some cleats for Lil Bobby.

Me: Ok cool. Lemme find out that's yo' lil boo thang now.

I texted her back, joking with her.

Xavier was a classmate of ours from high school that now coached the local little league football team Kitty's son played for. I knew that my friend was crushing on him, and I didn't blame her. Even though he was a hoe back in his school days, he was a good dude now. Damn near all the football moms wanted a piece of that fine ass chocolate man, but he only gave into Kitty. She brushed him off like she wasn't interested, but it was clearly evident.

No one bedsides me and Xavier knew about the old school fling we had with each other back in the day. We were cool and he didn't see me as anything other than a classmate. I'd always had a crush on him myself, shit. We fucked around a couple times after the day I lost my virginity to him, then he cut me off being that he was scared to sneak into my mother's house. We attempted to fuck outside behind the house, but our nosey ass neighbors were always watching and ready to report some shit to my mama.

Soon, Kitty gave in to Xavier's advances, and they became official. When he moved in, I told her that I felt that it was time for me to find a place to go because she officially had a man now, but she didn't want to lose her guaranteed hair dresser, chef, maid and babysitter. Xavier and I didn't start messing around until Kitty hosted a New Year's Eve party at her crib. Xavier was looking sexy as fuck as usual and after all the guests had left, Kitty was passed out on the couch, slobbering out the mouth in a vodka induced coma. Her two kids, Lil Bobby and Briana, were knocked out sleeping in their rooms.

Full of that Hen dawg, Xavier was in the kitchen tripping over his feet as he attempted to clean up the mess he made after drunkenly trying to fix himself a plate of nachos I had made earlier. Since I was still up after waiting for my booty call that stood me up, I decided to help him, so he wouldn't hurt himself. I mean, I was the freeloading help of the house. Since we were younger, I'd never caught him looking at me in a sexual way. But this night, his seductive eyes slid across my body, turning my hot pussy ass on. I grabbed the serving spoon from him, finished fixing his plate then sat it on the table. I knew he was fighting to look at me. I could tell by his body language.

I should have felt bad coming on to my best and only friend's man at the time, but he wanted it just as bad as I did. Besides, I had him first. He was my first, so he would always have a piece of my heart and could always have a piece of this pussy anytime he wanted it.

Looking into his seductive eyes, I practically begged me to let me please him orally. I wasn't the little girl I once was, so I had more experience now. I knew how to suck a dick and take it all down my throat without gagging and no hands. I pushed him into the laundry room and closed the door behind us. I missed the feeling of his stiff, nine-inch rod that pleased me beautifully so many years ago. I missed it and I wanted it all to myself. I knew that Kitty's scared to ride dick ass wasn't doing this nigga right in the bedroom.

I dropped to my knees and pulled his jeans down with me. When his mushroom tip was at my eye level, my pussy leaked with satisfaction. Opening my moist tunnel, I took his flesh into my lips, massaging my tongue on his chocolate shaft that made me show off my nonexistent gag reflex. I had to remind this nigga who he was fucking with, and I was ready to show him what this pussy was made for. Plus, I knew that Xavier wasn't shit any got damn way. He acted as if he wasn't turned on by those homemaking football moms, but I knew that all men cheated. Yeap, every man but Barrack Obama.

I purred, matching his moans as I knelt down before him, looking into his hooded, romantic eyes submissively.

"You're secret's safe with me. I won't tell if you won't." I promised him with a mouth full of dick.

When I could taste his precum sprinkling on my tongue, I unbuckled my shorts, jumped up from my knees, hopped on top of the washer and spread my legs open, so I could take all of him deep inside my vacant kitty cat. He pulled himself inside of me deeply with every stroke, making my pretty pussy thank him in squirts. When the washer clicked to the spin cycle it gave his adrenaline the perfect boost to go into over drive bumping against my kidneys when he was sticking me. Rocking to the beat of his smooth strokes and the vibration from the machine, I erupted like a volcano. Our climaxes met each other just in time before we were interrupted by the sounds of Kitty's slurred voice coming from the living room.

With the quickness, I pushed him out of me, jumped down and smoothed out my clothes. Thank God there was a back door near the washroom for Xavier to escape out of. Kitty's footsteps drew near and the washer stopped just in time for me to pretend like I was pulling the clothes out.

"Hey, Miki. Damn them drinks you made had a bitch knocked the fuck out!" She slurred, wiping away the good sleep that dripped from the side of her mouth. *Oh, trust, I know.* I smiled sinisterly, continuing with the laundry.

"Have you seen Xavier?"

"Umm, not since earlier," I lied, brushing past her and hoping that she couldn't smell the pong of our badussy in the air.

***

After that wonderful night with our man, it only happened a few more times; mostly when Kitty was away at work or sleeping. Our secret was kept between us until Briana, Kitty's lil bi-curious daughter, skipped school one day and walked in on my ass bent over ass naked on Kitty's bed as Xavier was beating my pussy up. Her lil snitch ass couldn't wait to sing like a bird to her mama to help soften the punishment she had in store for her after finding out she was planning to sneak a boy in.

When my friend approached me and Xavier about us being found out, we both lied and of course she did what any other bitch in America does when they're forced to choose between a friend and a piece of dick. She chose her man, and I gladly left. Even though I was in the wrong for doing what I did, I never expected my only true friend to chose him over all that we built.

The years passed by and of course we lost touch. I stalked both their social media pages faithfully, envying him for being super dad to her two kids and their set of twins she recently had only three years ago. I also resented her for never reaching out to me just to see how I was doing. Kitty saw first-hand how the fucked up cards I was dealt set my life up for failure, and she gave not one fuck. So, fuck her, her perfect life and not so perfect marriage. Fuck Xavier too because he didn't care about the only son he knew for a fact was his.

I had a feeling that Kitty was the one who talked him into this paternity suit shit, but it's ok because I had to fight all my life, and I was prepared to fight for my fucking son if need be.

Chapter Three

Kitty

I stormed down the steps of Miki's apartment trying to hold my head up high, but deep inside, I felt so betrayed. Growing up, she was my best friend and I would've never thought she would do this to me. I've heard many rumors in the streets about Xavier having children outside of our relationship, but as long as it didn't come to my door, I wasn't tripping on it. We had just moved back to Houston when Xavier's messy ass cousin Monika reached out to spill the beans.

I was by that bitch nigga's side through the storm and won't no bitch gonna take my place and get more than me. I don't give a fuck if it was his son, I controlled by man and our money period. Seeing Miki after all these years brought back so many memories of what used to be. I tried to help her out many times before, and she repaid me by hiding some shit like this for all these years. I knew that my nigga wasn't shit, but he was still my nigga. I had no choice but to stay with his ass. Plus, he was paid, so he made sure me and mines were well taken care off.

Our kids were teenagers now, and I didn't want to start all over raising another small child. I just said that shit to shake Miki's ass up. I knew they had been fucking in the past, but I didn't think the baby was his until today when lil man came running through the door a spitting image of Xavier. She gave him the one thing I couldn't, a child of his own, from his flesh and blood.

J-Don

Nika: T'Asia is missing!

As soon as I powered on my cell, I had text messages hitting my shit back to back from my mama and Monika.

Baby girl was missing? Maybe that's why Nika came to Keke's house banging in the door like a mad woman. Then again, how the fuck she know where to find me?

I quickly answered my own question, remembering who I was fucking with. That psycho hoe probably had been following a nigga to Ke's house spying on me and shit. She needed a homegirl or something to keep her company, so she could stay the fuck outta my hair sometimes. I had a bond with Nika's daughter, so finding out this news at this moment, I didn't know how to feel. I prayed that we could find her, and she was ok. I had made up my mind that I was through dealing with my crazy ass gal and her games. Honestly, part of me wasn't sure if I could believe Monika right now. She stayed fucking with my emotions to get whatever she wanted from me.

I pulled my arm from under Keke, jumped up from my side of the bed and started getting dressed in a hurry.

"What's going on, babe? Is everything alright?" My boo asked, half asleep.

"Bae, I'm not sure right now. I just turned on my phone and got all these crazy texts from Monika about her daughter missing. I see my Mom's been hitting my line too, so I gotta see what's up."

"Oh, my goodness, Davon! Are you serious?" She shrieked, jumping up and calling me by my middle name as she always had since we were teenagers. "Do you want me to go with you? I just don't know what to do. I can't imagine what she's going through right now." She panicked, tears forming in her beautiful eyes.

"No, bae. Look, I'm 'bout to head to the house and call my mom's to see what's up. I'ma keep you posted, so don't stress about it, ok? Everything is going to be good, I promise." I pecked her lips when I finished putting my clothes back on and hurried out the front door to jump in my ride. I cared about Nika's daughter, T'Asia, like she was my own. Her sorry ass sperm donor didn't give one fuck about her. I knew that Monika loved to play games all the time with a nigga. A part of me felt that she wasn't just jivin' a nigga because she came all the way to Ke's crib.

I slid my cell out my pocket and dialed my mom's line. I could hear the hurt in her voice when she answered.

"J? J baby. Where are you? I-I just don't know what to do right now. Nika called and said that baby was missing. I just don't know what to do," she cried, stinging my heart.

I fought back my emotions as I skidded down the freeway. Forty-five minutes later, I was pulling up to my side of town. Goosebumps covered my skin at the sight of numerous police cars that were lined up in our driveway. This shit was really real. I couldn't believe baby girl was missing. If it wasn't one thing then it was another. The time I finally stopped fighting with myself about who I wanted to be with and this shit happens. I prayed that baby girl would return home safely and still had a feeling that Monika had something to do with her disappearance. I knew for a fact that she couldn't be trusted.

I jigged out my truck and slowly made my way up the driveway to where Nika stood next to my mother. I couldn't explain how she was feeling at a time like this, but she didn't seem to have the face of a grieving mother.

"J! I-I don't know where she could be or who would want to take my baby!" She screamed, running into my arms. It filled weird as fuck because we hadn't shown each other affection in years and the only time our bodies touched is when we were fucking.

I embraced her deeply, scanning my surroundings of the many pigs standing around, looking like they were staring dead at me. They knew who I was and the weight my family's name held. I looked over at my mother who could read the tension of my expression. She connected eyes with me and mouthed for me to just wait.

"Come on, Nika," my mother, Gail, said. "The detectives want to get some more information from you inside."

I let Monika go and walked side by side with her into the house. After making sure she was settled on the couch, I walked to the hallway bathroom to wait on my mother to finish her business, so we could chat a bit. She opened the door and pulled me into the bathroom. My mother was a woman, but she was also an Old G out here. She was married to the most hood nigga I knew, my father. So, she knew a lot of shit most niggas and bitches who claimed they lived the street life didn't know.

"Now you know it would've been better if you would've laid low from the house for a couple days," she whispered to me in a stern voice.

"I know, ma, but I was worried. Nika popped up at Keke's house all hysterical, banging on the door and shit at four in the morning." Mama put her hands up to Jesus and shook her head.

"I don't know, J, something just not sitting well with me. This shit is crazy. Have you talked to your brother?"

"Nah, not since the other day. That nigga been boo'ed up and shit. But don't worry, ma, the house is clean. Ain't shit here."

"Are you sure, son? If it is, let me know now, and I'll have Black come pick it up."

"Clean as a whistle," I promised her before she pulled me in her arms.

"Now you know the laws gonna ask questions about your whereabouts at the time she went missing. You got your story together?"

I could tell them the truth; I was deep off in some pussy with the woman I truly loved, or feed them a lie. There was no need to lie any more to anyone. Shit, Nika knew where the fuck I was because she pulled up. I just didn't want to involve Keke and those kids in nothing. *Fuck man!* I should've listened to my old man before he passed and stopped fucking with Monika's ass a long time ago.

Chapter Four

Malik

Watching the way Miki's body swayed through the door of the master suite hardened my piece in my pants. Mami was sexy as hell rocking a rose red Maxi dress that clung to her curvaceous body. I was more anxious than a groom on his wedding day. I've never met anyone like MiKisha, and I was ready to make things official between the two of us.

I had my loft decked out with roses and candles, even had some Ledisi playing in the background. Miki put me on last time we hung out. The time we spent together and the conversations we shared were the realest I've ever experienced. She knew of my past and never judged me. I had my Mom's looking into buildings I could purchase so Miki could run her own shop one day. She was a good woman, awesome mother and bad ass hair stylist. Her and Xavion deserved the world, and I was going to give it to them.

"Hey, boo," I greeted her, pulling her soft, warm body into my strong arms and pecked her lips. I opened my eyes when I could feel she backed away from me a bit. I could look at her and tell something wasn't right with her demeanor. I don't know who or what pissed my baby off, but they would be dealt with.

"What's wrong baby?" I dug into her thoughts as I led her to the couch to sit down.

"Nothing. Nothing at all." She shook her head, trying to hide her emotions. "I thought we were going out somewhere tonight?" she asked resting her head on my shoulder after sitting next to me.

"We can go wherever you want baby, in the morning, tonight I just want you to rest." I flirted with her, licking my lips and pulling her legs into my lap to massage them. I wouldn't say a nigga had a foot fetish, but I couldn't wait to massage them pretty motherfuckers and suck the glitter off them bitches. Everything about this woman turned me on and tonight, I wanted to make what we had official and make love to her.

"Oh, in the morning? So, you're kidnapping me for the night?" She cooed at me, softly moaning as I rubbed her feet.

"The night? Nah, bae. You ain't leaving this weekend." I laughed, making her smile. "If we gotta send Black to pick up lil man, that's cool, he can come too."

"Keke got her taxes and supposed to be taking the kids to Six Flags, so Xai ain't worried about me. I'm all yours, baby." She pulled her feet from me just as I was about to place my tongue between each of her toes and straddled me.

Looking me deeply in my eyes, she had a nigga's heart fluttering and shit like a lil bitch. She leaned my head to the side and attacked my neck, rolling her tongue across my flesh, making my dick stand at attention in my navy blue ballers. I wrapped my hands around her waist and hiked her dress up as our tongues wrestled in each other's mouth.

Before meeting Miki, you would never catch me kissing a bitch. That was something romantic and passionate. I didn't put my lips oh no bitch because they weren't my bitch, but MiKisha was my woman, so it was different. With her waist exposed, I could feel that Mami didn't bother to put panties on.

Fuck! I thought to myself. She knew exactly what she was doing to turn a nigga on. She had me right where she wanted me and right where I wanted to be. She continued to grind on me, teasing me with her hands wrapped around my neck.

"I missed you, Leek." She smiled before pulling my erect manhood from my shorts and dropping to her knees.

I slowly opened my legs to give her the room she needed to do her thing. Leaning my head back on the couch, I tried to hide the lone tear that dripped from my right eye. I felt like I was falling in love. Maybe it was the way Mami bobbed her head up and down and slurped on my shit like Pinky the porn star. I could feel myself coming close to spraying my unborn kids down her throat. I hadn't had any head since I was locked up from one of the crooked officers that worked ad-seg.

"Miki, Miki, hol' up, bae. Wait. Bend over!" I ordered her big facing her by pushing her forehead with my palms to move her away from my dick.

She hopped on the couch, taking the place I was sitting, pulled her dress over her head and tossed it to the floor. Seeing her pretty, glazed pussy smile back at me, I wasted no time undressing and sliding deep into her birth canal. Her pussy was even tighter than it was the very first night we fucked at the club. She reached behind her and pulled her ass cheeks open, begging me to slide deeper in her guts.

"Aaaahh. Leek! Right there, right there, baby. Explode in me, Daddy!" She screamed.

I gritted my teeth and tried to pace myself, hoping I could get a few more strokes in before I did as she commanded. I closed my eyes to take my focus off her fat ass that was bouncing back on me as she threw that jiggly motherfucker on me constantly. My niggas were just about to return to my sack to ensure me another round after I made

Mami rain on my pipe, but when Miki reached back in between my legs and squeezed my nut sack, it was over.

"Arrrgghh!" I growled like an animal, releasing my seeds into her massaging tunnel. I collapsed on top of her, struggling to catch my breath as she giggled and tried to peck my lips.

"Oh, this shit funny, huh?" I pecked her cheek then pulled her into my arms and laid her on top of me.

"Now if we're gonna be doing that all weekend, Xai ain't gonna be able to be over here," she laughed and made me burst out laughing.

We laid in each other's arms for about an hour in deep convo before I ran her a steamy bubble bath, bathed and massaged her to sleep.

I could get used to this shit. Who would've know that Malik Davis would ever be the one to be falling in love.

Chapter Five

Monika

I grabbed a towel from the bathroom cabinet, wet it under the running sink water and squeezed it under each of my self-made puffy eyes when I heard Jaidion's footsteps coming closer.

"Are you going to be ok for a couple hours? I have to go by my Mama's and check on her and the kids. Your Mom's said she's on the way back from Frenchy's, she went to go pick up some grub. Do you need anything before I leave?"

Staring at his reflection behind me in the mirror, I rolled my eyes where he could see it. Was this nigga fucking serious right now? At a time like this, he was going to leave me?

I told him ok in just above a whisper and watched him disappear out the bedroom. Granted since T'Asia had been reported missing almost three days ago, he had been comforting me by my side. But that didn't stop that nigga from texting his hoe and checking up on their secret family.

Since the night I went to the house my GPS had led me to, I hadn't said a word about my findings, and he hadn't either.

Having numerous detectives, news reporters and community members in and out of our house all week helping search for baby girl, I thought that I'd best keep playing the role of the hurt and grieving mother, so I wouldn't get found out. My nerves were getting the best of me. I constantly hoped and prayed that my daughter's body completely decomposed, and she would just go down as another missing child. It was a sad situation. What was even more sad was that J-Don was steady playing my dumb ass, and I was letting him.

My phone chimed from an incoming text message from Detective Martinez.

Martinez: I got some news for you babes. Can you talk?

With trembling hands, I responded then sat on the edge of my bed waiting for his call. With all the commotion that had been going on lately with the "search" for my daughter, I had completely forgotten that I snuck out to meet Martinez and give him the evidence I knew would put away Jaidion for life. I had love for that nigga, but I didn't care anymore about his freedom. He wasn't as "on" as he was when we first met. He let bitches and his baby mama knock him off his game. This nigga played the fuck outta me all the years, so it was time he sat down for a lil minute. Plus, I would be opening my boutique soon, and I didn't want him reaping the benefits of my business. I could just keep letting Estaban's old ass fuck me in my ass weekly and pay me then when I opened and made bank, I would pay him his lil 10% monthly and do me. Fuck J-Don and his hoes. Now he could see if they could be there for him like I was when he was doing time for his sorry ass father.

When my cell lit up, alerting me of his call, I snatched it up and answered it before it even began to ring.

"Yes. Hel-Hello?" I spoke from shaky lips.

"Now you know that any information I give you must not ever be spoken again, right? I know that at a time like this--"

I dropped my phone and stood stuck in my thoughts as I looked up at the news playing on the TV that hung on the wall in my bedroom.

"Just about twenty minutes ago, three fisherman were out alongside Bobby's Bayou. One of them discovered something other than the trout they were fishing for tonight when the fishing line caught onto a large foreign object that was later identified as a floating body. Detectives are arriving to the scene now to investigate further to see if this victim found is the body of young T'Asia Smith who has been missing for the past three days...

"Oh God! Oh God! they found her. They found that damn baby!" My mother screamed as she burst through my bedroom door.

I grew short winded, and it felt like my heart stopped. *They found her?* My life was over. That's the last thing I said to myself before I blacked out and hit the floor.

Chapter Six

J-Don

I pulled up to Keke's house and hopped out my whip. I know that I should be back at the crib by Nika's side with baby girl missing, but our home was too hot right now with all those people searching for T'Asia. I knew that the night I left fucked Keke up in the head, and she was still bothered about the things we had talked about because she had barely been responding to my text messages.

I banged on the door three times and no one answered. I knew she was home because she told me days ago she was scheduled off today. Plus, her ride was parked in the driveway and I could hear the kids running around the house.

"Ke! Come on, baby, please. What's up? Why you dodging a nigga, can we talk for a minute?" I shouted at the front windows I could see my newfound daughter peeking out from. I didn't know what was eating my babe, but she was tripping today.

My phone buzzed from an incoming text message.

Ke: Go be with your family and leave us the fuck alone! I'm done with your lying ass, nigga. And this time, it's forever!

I sprinted back to the door and started to knock again when I noticed some pigs sliding down the street in their famous HPD crown vics and changed my mind. I skidded down the driveway, jumped in my droptop and hit 288 with the quickness. I pulled out my cell and dialed Keke's line. As expected, she sent me to the voicemail twice. I exhaled deeply and dialed her up again as I took the next exit towards 610.

"What the fuck do yo' ass want. nigga?!" She shouted into the phone, sounding pissed the fuck off.

"Bae. What's up? Why are you tripping with me? I ain't lying about shit, baby. I've always been honest with you, now you know that boo." I didn't know why Mami was tripping, but this shit was ill to a nigga. Me and Ke didn't fight. That shit wasn't for us.

"You told me you hadn't touched Monika's ass in the last couple months-" she started and I cut her off.

"Babe, I haven't touched that girl. Man look, T'Asia was found missing and that's why I had to leave the other night. It's so many people running in and out that house, I haven't even slept and damn

sure haven't touched her ass. I told you what it was. It's just us, baby."
I knew for a fact that the whole H-Town saw baby girls' disappearance all over the news, so I didn't understand why she was tripping out on a nigga.

"Whatever, Jaidion! I'm tired of being your stupid little side bitch! I'm tired of your games and I'm so tired of you burning my pussy, nigga! Keep your dirty dick ass away from me for good. I'm done! Go stick that hot ass dick in some ice lil nigga!"

My phone screen lit up and beeped to let me know that the call had disconnected. I didn't even bother to reach out to Keara again because she had more than the right to be angry with a nigga. I had been fucking her on the side for years. Now when a nigga wanted to get his shit together and settle down, it was too late.

I rode in silence the rest of the way back to the house. My heart was filled with pain being that there was no update on baby girl, and the love of my life hated me again. I crept down the street and noticed that our house looked empty. For the past couple days, our driveway and street was lined up with cars from Equisearch volunteers, community helpers, news stations and detectives who assisted in the search for my stepdaughter.

As soon as I pulled into the driveway, I could see Monika standing near the garage with two suits beside her. One was taking notes while the other evilly stared at me as he held his search dog's leash tightly wrapped in his hands. I parked my whip, hopped out and ran to them, hoping for good news.

"What's up, Nika? Any update? Please tell me they found baby girl."

"Jaidion Davon Davis, please place your hands behind your back. You're under arrest for murder!" The officer who was taking notes barked at me before pulling my arms behind my back.

I grunted and tried to pull away from him but was unsuccessful. "Murder? Who the fuck was I supposed to have murdered?!" I yelled, drawing attention from our nosey ass white neighborhood.

The officer laughed again as he hauled my ass to the car. A scowl of confusion stained my face. My feet weighed a ton as I was shoved to the backseat door of the police car. The other officer, who held the dog just moments before, took off running like a track star when he lost control of his dog who had ran to the trunk of my car and started barking. I tried turning around to see what the fuck was going on. Everything was happening so fast. My stomach was churning with nervousness.

I ducked my head as the man shoved me into the backseat. With my hands bound behind my back in steel cuffs, my chest heaved up and down. I could hear my cell vibrating in my pocket, and I knew it probably was my mother Gail. I looked over at Monika who stood lifeless like she had seen a ghost or something as the officers popped the trunk of my car.

Murder? Who the fuck was I supposed to have murdered though? I thought to myself. All the niggas I bodied were accounted for and they would never be found, neither would the evidence, so I know these pigs had the wrong nigga. The longer I sat in the backseat cuffed and confused, the more pissed off I became.

I watched as the crime scene tech slid on a pair of blue, latex gloves. He took his time with a long, cotton swab and scrubbed my trunk. Next, he sprayed something into my car and when he hit the neon lights, the law looked back at me, shook his head, and I could've swore I saw a tear fall from the corner of his eye. The tech gathered all the evidence in a plastic bag, removed the gloves and placed them inside. Then he placed the bag in a black supply box before walking back to his van.

"Earlier tonight the young body of T'Asia Smith, the eleven-year old autistic child that was reported missing just three days ago from her home in Northwest Houston, was recovered when three fisherman discovered her body floating against the current at Sam Houston Springs lake, Bobby's Bayou..."

Hearing the news broadcaster on the radio say those words stung my heart. This crazy bitch! She didn't, she couldn't. All of a sudden, the small contents of my almost empty stomach came up and I was upchucking all over the floor of the police car. After finally catching my breath, I looked up again at Monika who now stood with a smirk on her face.

This crazy ass bitch killed her innocent daughter and framed me for it. I couldn't believe this sorry ass bitch!

Chapter Seven

Miki

Birds chirping and the scent of crispy bacon frying drew me from my sleep. I looked to the left of me and saw the bed that was once occupied by Malik was now empty. I unwrapped his expensive silk sheets from my exposed body, walked to his dresser drawers, and pulled them open in search for one of his shirts I could throw on to join him for breakfast.

When I pulled open the drawer, I saw a rectangular, black, velvet box with TV Johnny's inscription written across it in gold letters. I looked over my shoulder to make sure Malik wasn't approaching before I pulled the box opened. I was blinded at the site of a diamond encrusted tennis bracelet I knew costed more than anything in life I've ever owned. On the top of the inside of the box, the words, *Will you forever be my baby,* were stitched in gold letters that matched the ones on the outside of the box.

I grabbed one of Malik's folded, white tees and slid it over my head and arms before tiptoeing to the kitchen and wrapping my arms around his perfectly chiseled body as he made us breakfast. I ran my soft hands on his washboard abs, teasing him a bit.

"How did you sleep, boo? Are you hungry, baby?"

He turned around, pulled me into his strong arms and pecked my forehead. "I don't want them lips yet until you get that funk up outta there. Everything you need is already in the bathroom boo. By the time you finish, breakfast should be ready." He cracked up laughing and placed a kiss on my cheek before unwrapping my body. I snatched a fresh piece of bacon from the paper towel he aligned them on and tried to run off when he smacked me hard on my ass.

"A'ight, keep playing. Yo' ass gon' be in there moaning like you was last night!" I teased him. He cracked up laughing, and I ran when he pretended like he wanted to chase me.

When I made it back to his bedroom, I grabbed my overnight bag and headed to the shower to freshen up before breakfast. Feeling the steamy, soothing water spray from the wall onto my body was so relaxing. It felt good to have room to move around in the shower than the miniature tub I was used to back at my apartment. I could get used to things like this. A man that cooked for me and treated me as a priority was something I wasn't used to. I leaned my head back in the flowing water, drenching my natural curls. I decided to wear my own hair when I came over instead of one of the many wigs and weaves Malik was used to seeing me with. I needed that nigga to know that a bitch wasn't bald headed.

I tried to keep my mind off the unexpected visit I received from Kitty. It was amazing to me that almost eight years later, she wanted to confront me about her no good ass husband when that nigga had been secretly sending me money for our son the whole time. He told me that he couldn't be there physically but would always be there financially. Well, little Ms. Plastic build-a-body ass hoe must've found out about our little secret. I was going to get an abortion when I found out I was pregnant with Xai, but Xavier begged me to give birth to our child. He made it seem as if he would drop Kitty and the life they built to start a family with me. And like a young, dumb broad, my stupid ass believed him. I didn't know the first steps I needed to take to beat the custody battle I would soon be fighting, but I knew that I was gonna hop in that ring like Mike Tyson behind what was mine. Kitty and Xavier both had me fucked the hell up if they thought I wasn't.

As I washed my hair, I decided to ignore the pain I felt in my heart about my harsh reality and soak in the royal treatment I was getting from my new boo. When the time came, I would let Malik know about everything that was going on, but as of right now, I didn't feel as if we were serious enough to be in each other's personal business like that. I knew for a fact, after many men I dated, the last thing a nigga wanted was baby daddy drama. Malik had just been released from prison. I didn't need that nigga going back already.

I began to rinse the conditioner out my hair when I felt his strong arms wrap around my back, pulling me closer to him as he took each of my nipples to his lips and nursed on my breasts. His lips left my chest and traveled down to my not so flat stomach where he placed soft kisses. Then he began to peck the top of my cream box as he pulled my legs open on his face. He placed his index and forefinger inside my quivering kitty cat, massaging my pearl tongue that thumped in perfect pleasure. He lifted me onto one of the shelves that were attached to the shower. I panicked thinking I would fall, but he assured me that I was in good hands.

"I got you, baby. You good, trust me."

He tightened his grip on my thighs and went to work tickling my creamy insides with his massive tongue that had me about to drop a tear from my eye. He kissed, nibbled and sucked on my juicy flesh as I palmed his waved up taper fade, trying hard not to punk out like a lil bitch. I started to grind on his face and fuck his nose as my pussy squirted in his face, thanking him. The more he squeezed my ass and devoured me, the more I rubbed my shit all up in this nigga's nose. *Got damn, who taught yo' ass to eat monkey like this nigga?!* I thought to myself, constantly moaning, ignoring how steamy the bathroom had gotten since we started.

I pushed him off me, turned the shower off and hopped out as he stood confused. "It's getting hot in here, let's go to the bedroom!" I shouted at him.

I was trying to run off when he snatched me up, bent me over onto the bathroom sink and slid his inches far past my birth canal. I was mesmerized watching this thug as nigga beat my back in in the mirror as he gritted his teeth staring back at me. I closed my eyes and let him finish doing his thang. When I was fucking, I had no other cares in the world. It was like sex temporarily took away all pain; it was my drug, I was addicted to dick and the way it made me feel. Even though it had been a lil minute since I fucked something, I was enjoying every single moment of this. I deserved it.

His strokes soon slowed up and I could see him squinting his eyes. "That's right explode in this pussy, baby," I cooed to him, turning him on even more.

He tightened the grip he had on my hips, exhaled loud as fuck then slowly pulled out of me after releasing his cream deep inside my love box. He smacked my ass again then started to place kisses down my back, thanking me for this good pussy I packed around in between my legs.

Chapter Eight

J-Don

The whole ride to the police station, I was silent. I couldn't believe this fuck shit was happening to me. When the laws pulled up to the intake garage where I had been many times before, I felt like karma was coming back to kick me in the ass.

Four Years Prior

I sat across the table from the bald headed detective who continued to drill me on Wolf's assault.

"So, you mean to tell me that you, Jaidion Davis, were not seen at Shivers Park on Wednesday evening, beating Thyrone Samuels like a runaway slave?"

I sucked my teeth at him and pursed my lips, sliding my hands into the pocket of my hoodie. My mother was outside waiting on my lawyer, Jacobs, one of the best that practiced in the dirty south. I was taught at an early age never to talk to the police. I just sat there and stared back at their no information having ass as they tried to get info from me. I know that me handling Wolf's ass in broad daylight was dangerous, but at the time, so much fuck shit was happening in a nigga's life that I had to handle business. My father was gone, I almost lost my girl, and my family blamed me for everything. I was numb inside, so I had no feelings about shit.

"Ok, that's fine. You don't have to talk to us. When the ADA gets here and throws those twenty-five years to life at your ass, then you gon' want to talk. But then it'll be too damn late. This is your third strike, huh?" The bald detective laughed and shook the table like I was gon' fold like a punk bitch or something.

"Detective Williams, can you tell me if your superior, Captain Jones, is in?" My lawyer, Jacobs, asked, making his presence known when he entered the room. I sat back and exhaled. I knew I was in good hands. "Tell him to come holla at me. I need to know why my client is continuing to be interrogated after he's spoken the magical words that explain why I am here?"

"It's ok, we're gonna get you, nigga. You and your family. We've been watching you," The other Detective Martinez reminded me before they exited the room and left me to chop it up with Jacobs.

"Alright, J, I'ma be honest with you. It's not looking good. Now nigga, how many times I done told you about controlling your damn temper? You can't be murking niggas all willy nilly in the open like that!" He barked through clinched teeth. Adam Jacobs was a white boy from Brooklyn New York, so he had a hood swag to him. This blonde hair, blue-eyed motherfucker looked like an off-brand version of the infamous Tommy off Power. He acted just like that crazy ass nigga too.

He was a slamming ass lawyer that stayed undefeated. Nobody was fucking with this nigga in the courtroom. Our father kept him paid to keep himself out the penitentiary. And when Big Ken was on the verge of his third strike for murking niggas, I served his time for him. Now look how the tables turned. Here I was, facing my third strike, possibly facing life in prison, all because my dumb ass was torn between my bitches.

If Keke wouldn't have been tripping on a nigga the other night, I wouldn't have gotten caught at my baby mama's house. I needed to just face it and stop blaming other people for my actions. I was gonna miss the fuck out my kids, but I did this to myself. So, even though I was gonna have to see my kids through a glass, fuck it.

"J! Are you hearing me, dude?" Jacobs shouted, pulling me from my thoughts of despair. "They just picked up your brother. An eyewitness identified both of you that day of Thyrone's assault. Now your girl called me earlier and presented me with this. If we get your brother to take the charge, we can persuade the ADA to drop the charge from murder to manslaughter. Since he will be a first-time offender, he would only have to do at least two years and can be back home in no time. Now you, on the other hand, will be looking at nothing less than a dub to life."

Shit gets real when you see them numbers on that paperwork. I learned from an old school nigga the last time I was in jail that kept reminding me how important it was to do your own time. Every time I went to jail, it was for my bitch ass father. Even though I was the oldest, Pops always treated my lil brother, Malik, like he was the right-hand man. I know I was in the streets goofin' sometimes and

*trickin' wit' bitches, but I could handle bit'ness too. Shit, maybe it
wouldn't be bad if Malik sat down for a minute. He was young with no
kids and had his whole life ahead of him. I didn't want to sell out my
brother, but with him sitting down for a lil while, that would help me
get my paper up in the streets a bit.*

*I made many sacrifices for my family on behalf of my father. It
wouldn't hurt lil bro to do the same for me.*

The laws hauled my ass into the same interrogation room I had
visited many times before. I knew not to say anything because I was
sure my mother and Jacobs were on their way downtown to meet me. I
couldn't believe that I was being charged with T'Asia's murder.
Seeing the crime scene unit pull evidence out the trunk of my Camaro
while Monika stood emotionless churned my stomach.

This hoe was really mad about me not wanting to be with her
bitch ass anymore. Shit, I felt stuck with her. We weren't evolving, we
stayed arguing about every little thing and our business didn't start
rising up until Malik came back home a couple months ago. Monika
didn't even make my dick hard anymore. I just fucked the bitch to shut
her up. When I was with Keara, we made love, *real love.* I couldn't
help that's who my heart wanted. The only reason why I fucked with
Caresha was because Keke refused to commit to a nigga time and time

again. Many bitches acted as if they didn't want a street nigga, but they wanted the funds that came from hustlin' tho.

I sat down and stared blankly at the wall that was facing me. I knew it would be best if I kept my cool. For once in my life, I was innocent. I would never kill a fucking child, especially one I loved as my own.

"Jaidion Davis! Long time, no see, brother. They say old habits die hard, huh? Well, I must say that I would've never guessed that you were the one responsible for the demise of your own father," said Detective Martinez, who I recognized from the streets and the previous time when my brother got locked up.

I cocked my head to the side and gave that nigga a confused look. Shaking my head and licking my lips, I asked him to reiterate the shit he just spoke. "What the fuck you just said? I supposed to had did what?"

He smiled widely as his partner entered with a file box full of "Evidence".

"I said we got yo' ass, nigga. For years, the murder of Kenneth Davis was unsolved. You pretty much had us fooled thinking that the truth about your father's death died with Wolf. But the truth is, you're the one that pulled the fucking trigger." He laughed as his partner began opening the box and pulling shit out.

"I wonder how your lil brother, Malik, is going to feel knowing that he took that bid for your lying ass."

"Man, nigga, you got me fucked the hell up!" I barked at his bitch ass, shaking the table. He better be lucky both of my hands were cuffed because I probably would've choked that bitch as nigga. "Ay, I know my lawyer and my moms sitting outside. Tell Jacobs to bring his ass in here. I don't have shit to say to you bitch ass pigs, man."

"That's fine, lawyer up. But this time, your family's usual hefty contribution won't be able to bribe anyone to lose this evidence that was handed to us."

They exited the room and my lawyer came in with no emotion in his face. "Hello, J," he greeted me very awkwardly. I could tell that something wasn't right with this nigga. My stomach started churning as he sat across from me, pulling paperwork from his Gucci briefcase. "Once again, it's— it's not looking so good, J. I really don't know if I want to take on this case because I honestly don't know if we could beat this—"

"Fuck you mean, you don't know if we can beat this?" I mocked him, growling and clenching my teeth. "I didn't kill my fucking old man. And if you in here to tell me these hoe ass laws done tried to cook up some fake ass evidence to prove otherwise, you must be hitting them daily Booga sugar packs super hard homie."

I watched him swallow the large lump that sat in his throat before he continued. Pulling out two manila folders and placing them on the table in front of me, he opened them slowly, one by one. I scrunched up my face as my eyes burned red with fury. Sitting there just inches away from me were pictures of the same gun Monika took from my hands the night I contemplated shooting my brains out. This grimy ass bitch! That hoe had me turn against my father, my family and kids just so she could set my dumbass up.

I became so irate that the next thing I know I lifted up from the table forgetting my hands were attached to it and tried to throw it against the concrete wall. I needed to see that bitch. I wanted her dead. She was a nothing ass hoe, and she needs to fucking die tonight. How dare that bitch go against the grain? I gave that lil pissy, loose ass pussy hoe a life after her sorry ass baby daddy pushed her and baby girl to the side.

"Calm down, Mr. Davis, or we will have no choice but to sedate you!" An officer yelled. I turned around and saw the weary face of my mother who stood outside the interrogation room with dried tears on her face.

"I didn't do this shit, Mama. I promise I didn't do this shit man. That bitch Monika is framing me!" Was the last thing I yelled out before the laws hauled my ass off to a padded solitary cell.

Life was so fucked up. A nigga really couldn't believe I was going through this shit.

Chapter Nine

Malik: We might have to cancel our plans tonight, love. I got some shit going on with my brother. I'm so sorry, boo.

Me: That's cool. It's ok. I hope that everything is fine.

I was a little disappointed that Malik backed out on our plans last minute because I wanted to spend time with him. When we were together, it seemed like I had no worries in the world. He took my mind off of my own personal issues, but I also understood that family business came first.

It was almost noon and since I had no clients today, Keke told me that she would be coming by so we could chat a bit. I didn't mind because she was really the only friend I had. I had been spending so much time with Malik lately, we hadn't really seen or talk to each other, so it would be good to catch up. I asked if she wanted to hit up one of her favorite spots for Happy Hour, either Boudreaux's or Don Pico's, but she refused. So, I just decided to pull out my Ninja blender and whip up a couple Crown Royal Peach coladas.

Malik: Please don't be mad at me, baby. I'm sorry.

The last thing I wanted was for him to think I was mad.

Me: I'm not mad, baby, I just miss you. Well, I miss that pipe. lol

Malik: He miss you too, boo. If I finish up early, I can send Black by to scoop you and lil man and bring y'all to the crib if you'd like. I'll be in late, but y'all can order some pizza 'til I get there.

Me: Ok, I'll let you know. Keke is on her way, so I'll hit you up after she gets here.

Malik: Ok, bae, that's a bet.

As soon as I finished reading Malik's last text and began to pour our glasses up, Ke appeared at my screen door. I sped walked to the door and unhooked the latch to let her in.

"Hey, boo. what's going on?" I embraced her tightly in my arms after seeing the distraught look on her face. "Have you been crying, boo? What's going on?" She couldn't even get her words together as I led her to the couch. "Here, love. Have a seat. I made us some drinks. Relax, boo, and tell me what's been going on." I tried to calm her, but I felt that it would be best if I just waited a few moments for her to catch her breath then lace me up with what was going on.

"I'm going to fucking helllllll, Miki!" She cried, lifting her daiquiri from the table, almost spilling it. I grabbed it from her hands and sat it back on my coffee table.

"I can't-- I can't believe I killed my baby. Oh Gawd!!!!!" She cried and screamed again. I ran to the kitchen to grab a few paper towels then returned to the living room and wiped away her snot bubbles that were forming from her face.

"Ke, what baby? Take a deep breath, breathe out slowly, then tell me what happened babes."

I watched her inhale then exhale. She sniffled again then sat back on the couch looking at me with so much hurt in her eyes. Keke was the first friend I made since I've moved to Fifth ward, and I've never seen her upset about anything. To see her hurting hurt my heart.

"Bitch, I'ma baby killer. I had a fucking abortion. But I had to, Miki. J-Don's lil dirty dick ass burnt me bitch!"

I almost dropped my glass on my project tile floor when she let that cat out the bag. "Wait...who?!"

"Bitch, Jaidion Davon Davis Sr., hoe, don't judge me." She finally laughed after cutting her eyes at me.

"So, all this time you been sneak fucking J-Don ass and wasn't gonna tell me nothing? Girl, you ain't shit!" I pulled her back into my arms to make her not feel so bad about herself.

"Bitch, yes, that's who I been fucking. He ain't nothing but a hoe, and that's why I didn't want anybody to know I was fucking with him. Now after all these years of sneak fucking, the secret's out. I'm too through with his nasty ass though. Bitch, I ain't never EVER had my coochie on fire. Usually we use rubbers, besides the time I got pregnant with Kasey, but that nigga caught me slipping when I was drunk, and a bitch got burnt and pregnant. Now he locked up for murder and our fiery seed is sitting in a jar of saline down at planned Parenthood."

My eyes bucked. I removed the straw from my glass and took that shit straight to the head. This tea was too motherfucking hot. I didn't get in Monika's personal business, and with Malik's text earlier, I now had an idea of what was going on. I hadn't spoken to Monika since the last time I touched up her hair a couple weeks back. I heard from Ms. Jackie about the child that was reported missing, but I didn't watch that depressing ass news. Houston was a large city and it was always some bull shit going on. I figured my life was more peaceful without tuning into that madness every day at five o'clock.

"Girl, it's just too much going on with that nigga. He needs to stop calling me from the county, bitch. I'ma block their number."

"Girl, whatever, you know you love that nigga's spicy ass dick. That was fucked up what he did, but maybe his girl burnt him?" I raised a messy eyebrow in her direction, thinking about the pills I found that day at Monika's in the guest bathroom. That explains why Ke had a lil fishy smell that day. That happens when you fuck dirty community dick. Trust, I know. Xavier kept my ass itching and burning, walking in the clinic bowlegged because I couldn't close my legs from scratching my flesh to the white meat.

"Most of us been through it, but hold your head up, boo. It's ok. Shit, at least you had the courage to go see what the fuck was going on with your body and get your results, plus get treated. Many of these hoes don't even wanna bust it open for the OBGYN, but will bust it open faithfully for a nasty ass nigga. You good with me, boo."

"Girl, that nigga just got way too much going on for me right now. I just don't know what the hell to do. Bih, I ain't never had a fucking abortion."

"Wait, you said he was locked up for murder? Who that nigga murked?" I inquired messily.

"Miki, I don't even know. I told you that I haven't been answering his damn calls. That's what my ass gets for trusting his nasty ass, again," she mumbled, shaking her head.

"Ke, now don't hold your head down about shit. You have no reason to. You're beautiful, smart and a great mother. You have your own hair that's yours. So, hold your head up, queen. We're gonna get through this together. Alright?" I hugged her again, and she finally dried up her tears.

"What nigga!?" She screamed into her phone. "I'm on my way down there now. I'm leaving your hood. No. Nawl, nigga, I don't wanna hear them lies. I'm on my way. Goodbye."

I stood with my back against the island in my kitchen with folded arms, shaking my head. I put my hands up in a surrender position when Keara looked my way.

"Now you know I don't judge," I reminded her as she grabbed her bag and her drink and headed to the door to exit.

"I'ma call you later, boo. Thanks for letting me vent, Miki."

We said our goodbyes and seconds later, I was heading down the stairs when Ms. Jackie rang my line. Any time she called, I never answered because I knew she wanted or needed me to do something, so I would just hike it downstairs to see what I could assist her with.

I tapped on her screen door twice before a tall, dark skinned woman with a matted old ass quick weave pulled the door open. She looked me up and down, and I returned that shit right back to her mangy ass.

"Yes ma'am, Ms. Jackie, do you need something?" I brushed passed the rude broad who was still standing at the door and made my way across the living room to where my neighbor was sitting in her recliner watching her daily stories.

"Excuse my daughter, Lashay. She acts as if she doesn't have any home training. Shay. this is Miki my neighbor. She helps out a lot with that boy of yours and she be helping me fix my wigs sometimes. You should be thanking her," Ms. Jackie scolded her daughter matter of factly.

"Mama, don't start yo' shit." Lashay darted her eyes at her ill mother than smiled at me while sitting down on the sofa parallel to where her mother was seated.

"I hope Jordan don't be giving you any trouble," she started, pulling out a swisher cigar and beginning to break it down.

"No. he's a sweet child. *Very respectable*," I emphasized, giving her a hint that she definitely was not. "My son, Xai, and him are best friends. Is there something you needed, Ms. Jackie?" I asked, trying not to show the way my nostrils flared up being that I was highly agitated with her daughter's foul ass presence.

"Yeah, Baby. I called you down to give you some change for fixing my hair for church last Sunday. I told you I told you I was gonna put something in your pocket when my lil check came. Shay, gon' over there in the room and bring me my purse please," she ordered her daughter, who's disrespectful ass straight ignored her the first time and continued to roll up her weed.

I swallowed the lump that sat in my throat and tried hard to change my facial expressions that I'm pretty sure were evident as they always were. No matter how hard I tried to hide how I was feeling inside, it showed clear as day on my face.

"No need to do that. I told you that you're good, Ms. Jackie. You help me out a lot with Xavion, and I appreciate that to the fullest."

"No. No, Miki. You gon' take this lil change," she insisted, ordering me not to leave until her daughter, who was now digging in her purse, sliding crispy Jacksons in her pocket, brought her purse. "I know how it is raising babies by yourself, that's why I try to help you and my daughter even though she ain't worth half a damn." She cracked up laughing then began to cough uncontrollably. I walked to the kitchen to grab her a bottle of water from the counter that her daughter snatched from me.

"I got it, boo. Don't listen to nothing my mama say, she's old. I do take care of my son, it's just not easy, you know. I don't have a baller like Malik Davis wining and dining me daily."

My eyebrows furrowed. How did this chick know about me and my new man and this was the first time I'd ever met her?

"Yeah, my homegirl Myia be fucking with him. She said that he went all out for you on y'all lil date at the suite downtown or whatever. Roses, candles and all that shit. Must be nice to be a H-Town baller's number one bitch!" She sneered, returning to the living room with her mother's purse finally.

"Mmm mmm. That's a damn shame about what they did to that baby. I'm glad they found her though. She's in God's hands now." Ms. Jackie stared at her TV with wide eyes.

"How much you want me to give her mama?" Lashay asked, steady rumbling through her mother's purse.

"Bring it here, I said! I don't want you digging through my shit again. I was missing my light bill money last month. You need to stay off that damn dope," she scolded her daughter who sat her purse in her lap then flopped down on the couch lighting the tip of her weed.

"They tryna charge J-Don with doing that to that baby, and I saw Monika's ass dumping her in that water. Them laws gon' catch up with that hoe sooner or later."

"*Detectives are saying that water was found in her lungs, meaning this young child was thrown in the water while she was still alive....*" The news broadcaster stated making my eyes widen and heart drop.

"She was still alive?! They could've saved that damn baby!" Ms. Jackie shrieked.

I stood stuck in my stance until Lashay brought me out of it by handing me over the five, crispy twenty-dollar bills from her mother.

I thanked her, said my farewells and headed back up the stairs. I knew that Lashay was in the streets deep, so she could have just been talking out the side of her neck, but what if she was right? What if Monika really did harm her child? The few times I did her hair, I would never see baby girl. I didn't know her on a personal level and never wanted to.

Ring Ring!

My phone's ringtone snapped me out of my thoughts.

"Hello?" I answered, wondering who could be calling me from an unknown number. I usually didn't answer calls like this, but after the hot tea that just got spilled in front of me, I needed something to take my mind back to earth.

"Miki. Hello? Are you busy right now? Can we meet somewhere and talk?" I rolled my eyes and desperately tried to hold in my scream I wanted to let out. It had been about four years since I heard his voice, but I would never forget it. How dare he reach out to me at a time like this? I sat back on the couch and rolled my eyes.

"What the fuck do you want Xavier? And why the fuck are you calling me from a restricted number?"

Chapter Ten

J-Don

I slammed the phone on the receiver for the fourth time today. I hated that my mother was dodging my phone calls. It hurt like hell knowing that the only two women who always have been on my side, Keke and my mama, currently didn't want a damn thing to do with a nigga. When I sat in that interrogation room with my lawyer the other night, I felt like that nigga knew I was guilty too. Truth is, I did not kill my own father. Yeah, we bumped heads often when he was still here and that's because I was stubborn as fuck. Pops always tried to preach to me just how important it was to build our hustle up before trying to settle down and have kids, but he wasn't practicing what he was preaching.

So, since I always was a sucker for love, I slacked in the streets to start a family. Now look at how this shit was coming back to bite a nigga in the ass. I'm glad Keara finally answered my calls. Hopefully, I could get her to talk some sense into my mother and make her come to my side again. I didn't even bother to reach out to my brother because I knew that after the evidence was thrown on the table, the same gun that was used to kill Wolf killed my father. Yeah, it was one of my guns, and the only person that had access to any of my weapons was my girl. After the laws searched my trunk that night and pulled out evidence about baby girl, I felt that my life was over.

Being that I had considered that lil nigga Wolf as one of my lil homies, I looked out for him, taking him under my wing and teaching him the game when none of the old G's from his hood wanted to be bothered with that nigga. I fucked up by lending his trigger happy ass one of my bangers. Shit, at the time I wasn't thinking straight. I had never used the gun before, so I let him hold it for me. The day I rode up on that nigga out there in the hood, I didn't have any weapons on me. I snatched the gun from him and started pistol whippin' his ass like a runaway slave. At first, I didn't even notice my brother was there with me until weeks later when the laws came looking for the both of us. I couldn't blame my Pops or the other Houston plugs out here that didn't wanna work with me. I was fucked up outchea, and I needed to start thinking straight.

I left the phones and walked back to the dayroom sitting area. Mugging the inmates that were crowded around a table playing dominos, I turned to face the TV's that hung from the ceiling in steel boxes. The news was playing again for the third time tonight and when I saw Monika's mugshot grace the screen, my dick rocked up.

"Aye, Boss man!" I shouted to the officer that was working my tank. "Can you turn this shit up some." He cocked his head at me and shook his head. "Please? Got damn!" I barked and he finally took his time walking his lazy ass to the control picket to grab the remote and turned up the television as I had asked of him. *Lazy motherfuckers didn't want to do shit*, I thought to myself.

"Just a few days ago, the petite body of young, T'Asia Smith was found in a muggy reservoir located just outside the Third ward neighborhood. T'Asia was a fourth grader at Sims Elementary school. Just days after her body was discovered, police received an anonymous tip stating that this woman identified as the missing child's mother was responsible for her daughter's disappearance. Detectives have tried contacting Monika Smith to no avail but haven't received a response. If you happen to see this woman, please contact your local authority's at 1-800-555-Tips...."

"Davis! You got a visit!" The short, stumpy, humpty dumpty looking fucker called to me, knocking my attention from the tube. I was nervous as hell seeing Keke at a time like this. All the times I was in and out of jail, she never came to visit a nigga because I didn't want her to see me like that.

"Step up for your pat search." I did as the female officer working visitation asked. After seeing that Monika's hoe ass was now on the run, I couldn't wait to chop it up with my brother and put a hit out for her hoe ass.

"Davis, go down to window number three, council visit."

"Council visit?" I said out loud to no one in particular. I was expecting to see Keke. But if my lawyer was coming with good news then I was down for it.

Sitting in front of the nasty plexiglass window that was full of only God knows what, my legs started to shake uncontrollably. Jacobs walking in with no emotion on his face made it no better.

"How you holding up J?" he spoke into the small holes that were drilled into the glass.

"I'm cool. Not really understanding everything that's coming at me right now, but hey, that's life, right. It's not really much to say when your own lawyer don't even believe you, huh?"

"It's not that I didn't believe you, Jaidion. Now, you know that we've been down this road many times before. I've made sure you and your father got the better part of the deal. But that's neither here nor there." He stopped his words abruptly with an attitude, pursing his lips at me then began to pull paperwork from his briefcase.

"Being that Monika is now in the wind, it's not so good because she is the only one that can testify the weapon that was all of a sudden found was indeed not yours at the time of your father's brutal murder. Do you happen to know of any of her family members or friends in any close states that she would have ran to for assistance?"

"I don't know of much of her family because they didn't fuck with her like that. I know she has a cousin named Xavier or some shit like that. I don't think he's in Texas anymore, but I'm not sure. Like I said, no one really fucked with her crazy ass like that."

"Ok, I'll look into it Baby Boy. Oh, by the way, do you know how Monika got ahold of the evidence the prosecution is trying to pin against you?"

I stared Jacobs in the face with clenched teeth, reliving the moment when that bitch planned this setup years ago. I leaned forward and told him to lean up so ear hustler's couldn't hear our bit'ness.

"That's what I snatched from ole boy the day I murked him. I ended up taking it with me in a fit of rage and when I got to the crib, Nika took it from me and "disposed" of it.

His eyes widened as he shook his head. "Boy, bitches ain't shit, I tell ya."

Smacking my lips, I agreed with him. "Tell me about it."

"Keep a cool head. I'll try my best to work this shit out. Hopefully, by the end of the week."

"A'ight, I gotcha."

He gathered his belongings, reminded me again to keep a cool head before we parted ways, and I was on my way back to my tank.

"Last call for visit! Evans, last call for visit! You don't bring your ass now then you won't get one 'til Tuesday of next week." A female officer bitched to another inmate. I looked up at the digital clock that hung in the TV room and saw that it was almost 8:30. I got excited earlier when I heard I had a visit because I thought it was my girl. I jumped up from my seat and made my way to the phones to call Keara again. I prayed that everything was alright. If she wasn't here within the next ten minutes, I wouldn't be able to see her until next week.

I gripped the phone tightly with sweaty palms as I waited on the prompts to finish and connect our call. I could hear heavy breathing and sniffling when the line connected.

"Ke! Baby, what's up? What's going on? Where you at, boo? I thought you was coming by to see a nigga."

"J, I'm at the emergency room with your mama. She— she's being admitted right now. She had a stroke."

Malik

My feet felt as if they weighed a ton as I forced myself to walk down the cold hallway. I couldn't believe my mom's had a fucking stroke. I had love for my brother, J-Don, but it seemed like that nigga was always fucking up, doing dumb shit and the family had to pay for it. I had no clue why that nigga was blowing up my phone from the county. I ain't have two words to say to his bitch ass. At this moment, I didn't know what to believe. Before Pops died, he told me to watch J-Don and them grimy ass east side niggas he did bit'ness with. I didn't trust them niggas, and I damn sure didn't trust him. I don't give a fuck if that was my brother.

Estaban and Big Black kept me laced up on the lil moves that nigga was making when I was doing his time for him. If I wasn't thinking about my nephew and nieces, that nigga would've been behind those concrete walls doing his time like karma had planned. But everything worked out the way it should because he was gone do his time now and I was going to make sure of it.

"Mr. Davis?" The charge nurse stepped into the lobby and called me. I jumped up from my seat and sped walked her way with the quickness.

"Yes, ma'am?" I greeted her with shaky hands. I got locked up just weeks after my father's death, so I didn't get the proper time to grieve properly. I couldn't take another parent passing, not at a time like this.

"Your mother is doing better now, and she's stable. Would you like to go in and see her?" I said a silent prayer and followed her closely to Ma's room. Taking a deep breath. I twisted the handle to enter the room. I walked in slowly, watching Keke feeding her ice chips from a plastic cup.

"Give us a minute, Ke, will you?" My mother spoke just above a whisper.

She placed a kiss on Mama's cheek then left us in the room.

I always will cut for Keara and my lil niece, but she was too good of a woman to be fucking with a low down ass nigga like my brother. I even told her that shit before.

Pulling up a stool to her bedside and leaning over to place a kiss on her cheek, she moved her head.

"Uh uh, son. I know you and my new daughter-in-law been getting it in. Don't put them lips on my face. You was locked up for a long three years." We both cracked up laughing, which made me feel good to know she was feeling a lot better.

"Yeah, we been doing our thang, ma. I'm ready for her to be mines, for real. I've been looking for houses and minivans and shit. I'm ready to play daddy outside the bedroom."

"Leek, yo' ass is a crazy fool. Just like your daddy, God rest his soul." Her eyes became glossy as she turned her head away from me.

"No, Mommy. Don't you do it. Stressing behind shit is why you laying up in here now. I'ma figure out everything that's going on. I promise."

"I—I just don't know, baby. What if your brother did indeed kill your father? I didn't raise him to be so got damn evil. I don't know who that child came from, but I know it wasn't my roots."

"Ma. I'ma handle it, ok? Don't worry about nothing. I'm finna head to Estaban now and see what's up. I'll call you with any information. I need you here and healthy so you can see me and my girl get hitched!" I joked with her.

"Alright, baby. You're right. Even though he ain't wrapped too tight, I still gotta love him. That is my child, just like you are," she reminded me, stroking the side of my face.

"You know, when you and your brother were younger, your father had many opportunities to get you all out the hood environment. But you know just how stubborn Ken could be. Jaidion is just like that father of yours and sometimes you are too. Baby promise me that you won't live this gangster life forever. I'm getting old now, and I want to at least see my baby boy become a father before the good Lord takes me home to glory."

I inhaled deeply and shook my head. Mama knew I hated when she started talking about her leaving the world. I knew the street life was tough, but she was married to one of the biggest plugs out here in H -Town. We were born into the street life and the dope game is the reason why she and our family lived so lavish.

"I know, I know. I can't say that I haven't enjoyed the lifestyle that it he has given me, especially knowing my children would never want for anything. But, there are days I would pray that your father would stop dibbling and dabbling out there in these streets and realize that he could go legit and do more with his life. I think when we both realized it, it was too late and had to come to an end. This should be a wakeup call for that brother of yours. He has children and you all have made more than enough for them to live a productive and successful life. Hang this street life up, baby, and do it before you become a father. You finally got you a good girl with a sensible head on her shoulders, leave this street shit alone. I'm selling the house and going to get me a one bedroom somewhere and a young boyfriend," She laughed, bringing a smile across my face.

"There is so much more to life than the dope gang baby. It's ok doing what you're doing as long as you're progressing. Grow from this shit. Your brother is just like your father, stubborn as hell. Now you, you have a chance to change your life, baby boy. You're still young with your whole life ahead of you. I don't want this shit to kill you all like it killed your father. Please listen to Mama, baby."

"I always listen to you. And I love you, Mama. Tell Ke to keep me posted. I'ma call you in the morning, get some rest."

"I love you too, son. And don't forget to bring me some breakfast in the morning before they discharge me. I ain't eating this shit."

"Yes, ma'am. I got you, boo. See you in the morning, baby cakes."

Chapter Eleven

Monika

"Fuck, Fuck, fuck!" I glanced at my mugshot that was staring back at me from the TV that hung on the wall of the bar as I rapidly walked past the window. I had just made it to Lake Charles, Louisiana and planned to escape to Florida if I could keep a low profile and stay under the radar of the pigs. I never thought that I would be on the run, but hey, shit happens.

I was pissed that Martinez's hoe ass didn't even give me the heads up that the laws would come looking for me. I should've known that any pigs couldn't be trusted. I really thought that I could get away with the accidental death of my daughter but Jaidion's stupid ass had cameras installed at the house. I was such a freaking idiot. I forgot all about that shit. Maybe if I would've reached out for help, I wouldn't be fighting for my life now. I was going down, so I was taking everyone with me.

Fuck that project living bitch MiKisha too. I put her broke ass on with a baller, and she didn't even care to reach out to me when my daughter was missing. I know that tired ass hoe saw that shit on the news. The first day she did my hair at her raggedy ass apartment in the hood and I saw her lil snotty nose brat, I knew he looked familiar. He was the spitting image of my big cousin, Xavier. So, I reached out to his wife, Kitty, and laced her up on her long lost friend. Shit, why not? That bitch didn't tell me that her homegirl Keke's black ass had been screwing my man all these years.

After I saw the footage from the club when them hoes jumped me, I recognized that Keke bitch. The night of T'Asia's death put two and two together. I stole off on Caresha, J's baby mama, thinking she was the one that was trying to keep me out of V.I.P., but it turns out that it was one of them lil dusty broads in Miki's click. After doing my secret spy research, I found out that bitch had been fucking my man for years.

That was bad for my ex-father-in-law, Big Ken. Ms. Gail, the Davis boy's mother, kept speaking ill of me and J's relationship, so I paid Wolf to dead that nigga. She wasn't there when that nigga was locked up doing time for her husband's fraud ass. Too many lil niggas in the hood worshipped Big Ken like he was a God or something. That nigga wasn't shit with his lil dick ass.

When I played like I cared about J-Don wanting to off himself years ago, the truth was, I really didn't give one fuck. I gave too much to his sorry ass and he repaid me by making me look like a fool in these streets. So, that nigga was going to pay for all the pain he put me through, including making me lose my son.

He claimed he cared about T'Asia, but he didn't. If so, he wouldn't have left that night and went to see about his bitch and their child. So, when he got back to the house, I had the laws waiting on his ass with the gun he gave me years ago that I knew had several bodies on it, including his father's.

I had about ten racks in my pocket, and that was enough to begin a new life. I didn't quite know what I was going to when I ran low on funds, but I would cross that bridge when I got to it. At this moment, I was just going to enjoy being on the run with no nigga, no responsibilities and no worries.

Chapter Twelve

Miki

Goosebumps filled my arms as I exited off the 610 south freeway. When Xavier called me earlier, I was surprised. I hadn't heard from his bitch ass since Xai was two years old. He knew what I was going through with my mama and still didn't give a damn. Yeah, I know I shouldn't have been fucking him because he was married to someone I considered my best friend, but he still had a responsibility as our son's father to help take care of him. I had a few words to say to his ass about his bitch showing up to my crib unannounced too. I pulled up to Dolly's Diner and parked in the back, waiting until I saw him to go inside.

He said he was coming alone, but if I saw his bitch show her long titty ass up, I was pulling off. I didn't have time for any drama in my life today. It was already enough going on. Plus, my mind couldn't stop thinking about the words Lashay said to me about Malik and his little bitch. I heard Lashay was a dope fiend, but she was a lil too detailed about me and Malik's date night downtown. So, either he running his mouth to bitches, or he got somebody stalking him.

I stared at my phone as it rang, showing Malik's number on the screen. When I saw a flashy ass, new model, Red Jaguar pull into the parking lot of the diner, I quickly hit the ignore button on Malik's ass. I waited a couple more minutes watching Xavier's long-legged, big forehead having ass hop out his ride, hike it inside the diner and grab a table.

Exhaling and rolling my eyes, I opened my door and made my way inside. Ignoring another call from Malik as I pulled open the diner's door, I slowly walked up to the booth Xavier was seated at and slid in.

"What's up Miki? How have you been?" He asked like everything was hunky Dory between us. I knew this nigga could tell by the mug plastered on my face that everything wasn't good.

"Well, our son has been great! Straight A honor roll student, he's playing ball now and being raised very respectfully by a wonderful single mother. And me? Well, I was doing good, living my best life 'til your wench of a wife showed her tired ass up to my house unannounced after making a fake appointment." I snapped at him, folding my arms. He started to say something and I cut him off.

"Hold up," I demanded, raising my hand as he raised an eyebrow, tapping his straw on the table and placing it in his glass of Dr. Pepper.

"You know what, Xavier, I don't know why, but I really thought you and I were better than that. How dare you send your bitch to my house to pull that ratchet ass move? Our son is seven! Seven fucking years old about to be eight soon." I spat through gritted teeth, looking him up and down as if he was nothing.

"So, when I stopped fucking you real good like you liked it, that's when you got ghost on our son, huh? Kitty can have you, boo boo. I'm glad I stopped fucking you when I did. You've been found out, homie. I know about y'all lil secret ,and I'm glad I dogged that damn bullet. I heard that yo' nasty ass gave her something she can't get rid of. She can have that life." I burst out laughing just to piss his pickle bump dick having ass off.

He sat back in the booth staring at me with eyes full of fury.

"See, that's the reason I stopped coming around. Look at your damn attitude, man. We can't even sit down at a public place and have a fucking decent conversation about lil man without you blowing the fuck up."

The waitress came to the table and asked us to quiet down. We both nodded to her then sat unmoving, staring at each other in silence for a couple minutes.

"I'm not hard to find, Miki. If you really wanted to find me, it's not hard at all. You be on social media flexing ya lil hair business and shit, you could've easily reached out for anything lil man needed," he stated matter of factly, sitting back on his elbows.

"You know what, Xavier? I've wasted my time coming here. We've been sitting here for how long? Almost twenty minutes and not once have you spoken our son's name." I laughed evilly. I didn't know who this nigga was trying today, but I wasn't his lil herpes having bitch. I wasn't the one, now or ever.

"His name ain't lil man, it's Xavion! I shouldn't have even given you that much power. When I was fucking with you, I didn't want to be a mother. I thought we were just having fun, but yo' punk ass cried for me to keep him just so you could neglect him his whole life? He's good without you like he's been the last almost eight years. And your lil bitch and her custody papers don't frighten me. Sign over your motherfucking rights, bitch. My son is great!"

I jumped up from the table and stormed out the restaurant with tears welling in my eyes. I couldn't believe I let that nigga take me out of character like that. I never said I was innocent, but I'd never thought in my life that he would try to take custody of my son. I'm the one that's there in the middle of the night] losing sleep when he's sick. Thank heavens for blessing me with a talent. I can work from home so I can make it to Xai's school events. And I won't have to worry about working crazy hours and miss out on his milestones. Fuck Xavier! I was done with that nigga and his bullshit, but I was always going to fight for my motherhood. Shit, it's all I have left in this cruel world.

"Miki! Damn, girl, you just brushed right passed a nigga like you didn't even see me. What's up man? What's going on and why are you ignoring my damn calls and texts?" I turned around to the familiar voice I knew and loved and met Malik's face.

"Boo, dry them shits up. I don't ever want to see you or my son hurting." He pulled me into his strong arms and began to rock away my pain.

"I'm just so tired of this shit. How dare he come at me sideways and ain't been there for his son? Fuck him! And fuck you too and your lil bitch Myia!" I pushed him off me and started punching his ass, laughing.

"You a stalker. How you knew where I was anyway? And why you ain't with your lil girlfriend?" I hissed at him, walking away.

"We not gon' do this shit because we don't do this shit. My dick ain't been in nobody but yo' thick ass, come here girl." He chased me around the parking lot and pulled me back into his arms where I felt so safe in this world. With Malik, I truly had no worries and I felt that I never would.

"I've been at the hospital with my Mama."

"Oh, my goodness, Malik! What's going on? Is she alright?"

"If yo' stubborn ass would've answered me then you would know that, huh?"

I stepped back, folded my arms and cut my eyes at him. He leaned forward and kissed my lips.

"Don't worry, baby. She's good now. She had a slight stroke but she's on the way to the house now. Stressing behind my fool ass brother. She just got discharged. You gon cook for me tonight?" He smiled at me, making me forget I was mad at his crazy ass.

"Nope, tell your lil girlfriend to cook for you." I snapped at him again.

He pushed me against my car, pressing his thighs against mine as he held my arms above my head. I could feel his steel hardening against my pelvis.

"Ain't nobody told you that messy shit but Lashay dope head ass. That's alright, I'll just eat this pussy! I already told you about Myia, so don't come at me like that for real boo. You the only bitch that's ever been to my crib or met my mama. So, stop it."

"Mmmnn hmnn."

"I ain't coming at you accusing you of being on a date with yo' punk ass sperm donor. Am I?"

I couldn't do nothing but roll my eyes.

"That nigga signed over his rights." He let me know, pulling an envelope out his back pocket. "And you and Xavion gon' be Davis' soon. Fuck that nigga, y'all good, love. Now let's go, I got some shit to show you." He walked me to the passenger side of my car and held the door open. After I slid in, he jogged around to the driver's seat and hopped in. I saw him wave to Black, his driver, as we pulled out the diners parking lot and hit the freeway.

I was really falling for this nigga. Since day one, he has shown me and my son nothing but the best. I'm so glad I met him.

Chapter Thirteen

Malik

I pulled up to the boutique in Pearland that was formally Monika's. Well, the shit was in my name and I was going to be using the business to clean my money, so it was mines. That no good hoe would soon be sleeping with the fishes, so won't shit hers anymore.

I parked Miki's whip, hopped out, then jogged around to open her door for her. Since the day we started getting serious, and I noticed the grimy shit Monika was doing out in the streets, like fucking my connect. I changed the locks on this place and started remodeling it and fixing it up to be the perfect salon for my baby.

"What's this place, boo?" Miki asked with wide eyes as we walked hand in hand into her shop. She looked around confused, trying to hide her excitement.

"A nigga gotta take a leak," I told her, hoping to distract the fact that Keara was pulling up with the kids.

I made my way to the restroom in the back, nervous as fuck, to wipe the perspiration from my palms. Reaching in my pocket, I pulled out the bracelet I got engraved for her months ago. I wasn't quite ready to propose or nothing, but I wanted Mami to know that I appreciated her to the fullest and what we had was really real. Walking back to the front of the salon, I saw that she had made herself right at home, pretending as if she was working behind a client in the chair. I tip-toed over to her, wrapping my left arm around her and placing the small velvet box in her hands with my other hand. Turning her to me, I swallowed her in my arms and placed my lips on top of hers.

"Bih, I told you! I told you that you would own your very own shop one day!" Keke came in screeching with the kids behind her, hands full of balloons.

"Baby, this shop is yours. All yours. And whatever you want to do with it, however, you want to decorate it, just let me know, and I'll write the check. You deserve it, baby."

Soon, my Polo tee was wet with her tears of joy. My future stepson came running up to us and joined in our family hug.

"This is-- this is so beautiful Malik, but you know that I haven't been to beauty school?" She cried, doubting herself, which I hated.

"Baby, what does that mean? This shit still yours. You're enrolling in school Monday and then you'll be done in no time. Quit doubting yourself. Now stand back so daddy can bling out ya wrist."

Monika

It seemed like everything I'd done in the past kept coming back to hunt me. Why was I such an evil bitch?

"Hey, what's up boo?" Wolf greeted me as he hopped in my whip.

"Hey, babe. What's up, let's take a ride". I entered the freeway lacing him up on my plan as he rolled up a square for us to smoke.

"Look, I got some shit for you to handle. All you gotta do is pull the fucking trigger. I'll take care of the rest--"

"Wait, ma. What the fuck?" He whined like the lil bitch he was born to be, cutting me off and agitating the fuck outta me.

"You said you would put me on working up under J-Don, so I could be on like them niggas. You ain't never said shit about me having to murk anybody. I don't know if I'm down with all that shit man, for real."

I took the next exit off the freeway and pulled into a gas station. Opening my legs, I pulled my sundress up and panties down. I took his free hand and slide it deep inside my cream box, bringing him back to reality.

"You see how wet she get for you, nigga? Even J-Don don't make her drip like that. So, if you want to be able to ever feel this good ass pussy again, I'd advise you to shut the fuck up and listen."

"Damn, baby. Shit let me taste that motherfucker fuck! You got my dick hard than a motherfucker, boo!"

I massaged my pussy with his hand to further fuck with him before pulling it out of me and licking my sweet cream from his shaky fingers.

"Now, you ready to talk business? Or you ready to get out?" I asked him with raised eyebrows.

It was amazing how a bitch's body could get her whatever she wanted in the world. A lot of these young hoes out here needed to get with the program and start using what they had to get what they needed out of life.

***

I had Wolf and his two homies camped out at a nearby hotel as I sat on Big Ken, watching his fool ass take care of business. He acted as if he was pissed about making this run for J-Don, but truth is, his lying, cheating ass had a family and young kids in Louisiana. After he fucked his second wife, he was leaving Lake Charles to head back to Houston with Estaban's new shipment, and that's when I made my move. While he was packing up the trunk, I snuck to the front of the car and stabbed his front tires with bails to ensure that he wouldn't make it far down the road.

Going on these weekly trips with my nigga, I knew the exact streets and back roads they would take to keep under police radar. I was on his ass like white on rice. Like clockwork, his caddy took a flat and made him spin off the road into the dark bushes where no one could see him right away. I called my hit crew, who were tailgating me, to run up on that nigga pistol first and snatch the dope and money off his ass. They were dressed out in jack-a-nigga gear, but I had nothing covering my face. I wanted Big Ken to see who would be firing the fatal bullets to end his sorry ass. After stripping him and the car, the crew hopped in the whip and got ready to speed off, but I noticed Wolf was standing over the nigga shocked and scared.

"What's up? You ain't man enough to pull the fucking trigger?!" I shouted at his punk ass, laughing.

"This ain't right, Nika. You said it was just some random nigga. Man, J is like my family, dawg. I can't do this bullshit."

"Move yo' punk ass out the fucking way!" I yelled at him like he was a disobedient child, snatching the gun from his waist and lighting Big Ken's ass the fuck up. My mouth watered with Glee, my nipples hardened, and I felt a small puddle form in the seat of my black tights as I watched his soul escape his body.

I had to end this nigga for all the hurt and pain he caused my man, making him do his time for him because his punk ass couldn't leave the streets alone. I had to end this nigga because Gail, the Davis boys' mother, could read me when she met me and knew I wasn't shit for her son. They stole years of J-Don's life and my son's by not wanting him to get out the game. I felt that my man could live a better and legit life with his sorry ass daddy gone forever.

"Nigga, take this pistol, hide it and get gone. Meet me back at the spot in Houston and I'll break the shit down and split it between *y'all. If I hear anything about you running your mouth about this shit that happened here tonight, I will find you, and I will kill you."*

I felt like the world was closing in on me. This on the run life was not at all what it was cracked up to be. I wasn't strong enough for this shit and it was time for me to face up to all the shit I've done over the years. It would've been easier trying to escape if I would've had someone on my side that truly cared for me. I was hallucinating. It seemed like every corner I turned, I bumped I to a little girl's who face matched my precious baby girl.

I called Estaban on my way to the boot, and he said he would be coming by to see me on his way to Florida. Every restaurant I passed, I saw the news playing with my mugshot plastered on the screen. I wish I would have never met J-Don, then I wouldn't have turned into this evil monster of a bitch. I really hated who I had become. I fought with myself silently over the years about the truth of my reality. I didn't deserve the good life J gave to me. Trying so hard to please a nigga and in the end, he didn't even give one hot fuck about my dumb ass.

"Mommy, Mommy. Come here!" I turned around and heard T'Asia's sweet, angelic voice call out to me. I walked over to her as she rocked back and forth on the swing with her baby brother in her arms.

I joined my children on the swing next to them, laughing and playing. I felt so at peace. I wasn't quite sure what was going on, but I felt like I had nothing else to worry about in the world.

"Mommy! Let's go to the water." Baby girl pulled my arm to the lake near the park.

"T'Asia. T. No, baby, come back up this way; it's not safe."

"But Mommy!" Her voice faded as she and her brother began to be covered by water.

I had to save them. I had to make this one thing right, then maybe God in heaven would spare me my well-deserved first-class ticket to hell. Following behind my children, my feet became wet, next my legs and thighs. Water was up to my shoulders, and I could hear voices around me.

"Somebody help her!"

"She's going into the swamp!"

I could feel my cell vibrating in the pocket of my jeans as my ears and eyes filled with water. I kept following my children until everything turned black. The feeling in my legs ceased and my heart stopped beating.

J-Don

"Baby. Baby. Listen to me, Nika!" I banged my fists on the bathroom door that she had locked herself in for the third time today.

"Leave, J. I'm tired of this shit, nigga. You outchea running with niggas that's out to get you and wonder why your family look at yo' funny looking ass sideways."

"What the fuck you mean niggas I'm running with?!"

I stormed out the house, hopped in my whip and tailed it to the Eastside with the quickness. I noticed that nigga Wolf had been dodging my phone calls lately, but I knew exactly where to pull up and find his simple ass. I'm not sure exactly who my girl was hinting at, but I had an idea because the Eastside niggas were the only niggas I fucked with like that.

I jugged out my ride, spotting that nigga sitting at the park smoking a sweet.

"Aye yo', homie. What up tho?" I raised both arms in the air to get that hoe ass nigga's attention. His eyes bucked seeing me foot it his way.

I ran up to that nigga like Carl Lewis and punched his unbalanced ass in the jaw, making him instantly drop to the cold, hard concrete.

"You actin' like a real lil hoe right now, hiding from a nigga and shit. I thought we had some bit'ness to handle? Nigga, stand yo' motherfucking ass up and step to me like a man!" I demanded him, yanking him up by his collar.

"Look, I ain't plan that shit, J. That was all your girl. She just told us that she had a lick for us to hit, so I was down for it. I didn't know it was yo' old man until after we ribbed that nigga."

I gritted my teeth so hard, I almost cracked my diamonds in them motherfuckers. My eyes burned red with fury, and I jumped on that nigga with no remorse. Snatching the pistol from his hands he tried to pull out on me, I beat that nigga's brains in until I couldn't breathe anymore. Someone pulled me back and tried to pull the heat from my hands, but I darted away from them, running to my ride and headed to the house.

My father! My motherfucking father! How could this hoe do this to me? I know that everything Big Ken did wasn't right, but I didn't plan on killing the nigga.

Fifteen miles and almost 30 minutes later, I pulled up to my mansion still holding the murder weapon I used to end that nigga Wolf's life. I couldn't believe that bitch ass nigga. He was my homie, somebody I fucked with tough out here in these motherfucking streets. But my father? My fucking father though. In the back of my head, I kept asking myself why? I would've appreciated if that hoe ass nigga would've come at me like a G, rather than orchestrating the demise of the only old gangster that gave a fuck about every lil nigga up under him. My father, Big Ken, was the realest nigga outchea in H-Town. Yeah, he was a street King that was from the hood, but he respected everybody in the game and they gave it back.

I jigged out the ride, darted to the front door and sprinted up the spiral staircase. I didn't stop until I reached the master bedroom. My derailed body slumped down to the floor, knocking over the nightstand that sat by our bed. Still clutching the heat in my right hand, I lined up the barrel with my right temple and squinted my eyes. This the first time in my life I had to end a nigga's life that I considered a friend. My father was gone, my brother and mother hated me, and my girl had just lost our child. I hated myself right now. I hated myself more than anything and the only person I had to blame was the man in my mirror.

"J! Jaidion! Baby, what are you doing?" Monika wept as she neared me. Seeing her big pretty brown eyes wet and full of hurt stung my heart even more. "J! I'm not going to let you do this! You've got kids to live for! Give it to me!" She squealed, holding out her hand which held a towel. "Give me the fucking gun. Suicide is not the answer. What do you think Big Ken would say to this? Yes, he is gone now, but your father was a prominent man. He left you and Malik so much more than just money." She knelt next to me. "He left y'all a fucking Empire! And you want to selfishly end what you've all worked so hard for like this?!" She screamed through trembling lips. "Yeah, nigga, you fucked up. Not only with me, but your father and the streets. You are still here for a reason so make it right. Don't punk out like a lil bitch because you hit hard times, nigga. Hold yo' fucking head up and rock that crown like the King you are born to be."

When she lifted my chin and stared deeply into my eyes that were flowing with angry tears, my heart melted. At this point in our relationship is when I knew she was my rider. I had just put her through some fucked up shit, and she was still here to help me through the pain.

Handing Monika the pistol, she wrapped it in a towel and set it on the bed.

"I'm sorry! I'm so sorry, Mika. I fucked up and I was wrong. If you leave me, I can understand. It won't be easy without you, but I can't even fault you, ma." I pulled her into my embrace tightly, and I was surprised when she didn't push away.

"I love you, J. I always have and always will. I'll get rid of the banger. Think about all the pain he caused you over the years and the time you did for him causing you to be away from me and our babies. I'll talk to Jacobs and see if we can work something out where your brother won't have to do much time then you can be the new Kingpin outchea. Your family has always looked down on you as if you were nothing in this game because you did something your father doesn't and that's putting your woman and kids first. I didn't want to do that shit to that nigga, but baby I had too, and I'm telling you that it will all pay off in the end just watch and see. But nigga I'ma make you pay for this weekend. Shit, you had me sitting up thinking the worse. Then on top of that, I lost our son. But I just helped you gain control of this empire. You owe me, nigga."

"I know, baby, and I can't argue with you on that. I don't want to fight anymore. I owe you everything. I owe you my life."

The buzzing of the cell tank door opening snapped me out of my dreams. I jumped up out my sleep, dripping cold sweat. I had been sitting in the county jail for three days and still didn't have any good news from my lawyer, Jacobs. I kept having this same dream over and over. I was being robbed and the jacking ass nigga shot me in the back of my head. This shit had me paranoid. I had a good feeling it was going to be Monika who would try to pull the trigger, but I stayed ready for that bitch. I'm not sure where the fuck Monika hoe ass was at, but she was staying out of dodge. Lil bro said he would reach out to Esteban and see if he could locate that crazy bitch, so I could go free. That nigga Ban could get eyes on anyone at any time.

"Davis! Get ya shit. You outta here, dawg!" The male officer called to me. I jumped up like a kid on Christmas, sprinting to the exit door with empty hands. I hadn't had much since I'd been inside, so I wasn't tripping on leaving nothing. I stood patiently as the officer cuffed my hands and slowly walked down the hallway.

"Step up to the glass window, and state your name. When you receive the plastic bag with your belongings, walk down to the locker room and change immediately. No talking, just walking. Let's move it!" The female officer shouted to me. I did as I was told without hesitation. After dressing into my clothes and signing for the rest of my property, I took the last long walk down the hallway to freedom, hoping to never see the inside of a jail cell again in my dear life.

When we were led out the last door that opened to the free world I saw Jacobs waiting for me outside, smiling. I pushed pass the slow walking inmates and made my way to his ride with the quickness. Jumping in the passenger seat, I tried to calm my nerves before asking the many questions I had for him.

"It's good to see you, J," He greeted me, turning off Franklin and heading to the freeway.

"What's going on? Man, I really thought that I wouldn't ever see the light of day again." My stomach started rumbling because I hadn't eaten much since I was locked up, and I missed the fuck out of my kids and Keke.

"Well, J, the case was dismissed. Something about missing evidence," he grinned, using air quotes.

"See, that's why I fucks with you, Jacobs. You know exactly how to get a nigga off." I dapped him up and took in the surroundings of the city I loved as he did 80 in a 60.

"Aye, you got any word on Monika's bitch ass? A nigga ain't trying catch no more bids, but I gotta see that hoe today!" I shouted in a fit of rage, thinking back on how she played me.

"She's dead. The psycho bitch walked into a swamp full of Gators the other night." Jacobs laughed loudly, making me scrunch my face up.

"Gators? What the fuck?"

Malik

"What's up baby bro? We still meeting with your boy today?" J asked when I answered my cell.

"Yeah, that's cool. I'm pulling up now. About what time you gon' pass by?"

"In about another fifteen minutes."

"Bet."

I ended the call and met Estaban inside the warehouse. "Aye Papi. What's good? You ready to do this?"

"As ready as I'll ever be!"

"Well, let's have a drink to celebrate, and I'll see you when you finish."

We toasted a couple shots of Hennessy Pure White in the air and when J-Don arrived, it was time to get down to business. He walked in excited, smiling like the Kool-Aid man and running his hands together like Stevie J's rat looking ass. I told him to take a seat across from me so we could get down to bit'ness.

"Ay Leek, I thought that nigga Ban was joining us?"

"He had to go run and take a leak. He'll be back in a minute."

"A'ight, cool. Let's get it."

"Yeah. Let's just get down to bit'ness."

"Sometimes you can want something so bad in life that you're willing to do just about anything to get it. Even putting your family and loved ones in jeopardy to fulfill selfish desires. I've always thought Pop's death was an inside job. No one ever knew exactly where our out of state connect was but the three of us. Ma never even knew and didn't have one earthly idea until his body was found. I've had time plenty of time on behalf of you, my brother, three long years to be exact, to sit and think what would ever make a nigga cross his one and only blood brother? The way we were raised up, it's been nothing but pure love between us. You know what's some fuck shit though, J? You're a hoe ass nigga in my book. You wanna know why? Yo' bitch ass sold your soul to some Eastside niggas for popularity thinking you was missing out on some shit in your own damn hood. Was the grass really that greener to make you kill your own father? Pops talked about you constantly saying out of the two of us, he knew I was the one he would never have to worry about. You should've been concentrating on grinding to get to the top of your own hood. Instead, you chose to put niggas and bitches you lived to floss your money in front of before your own family. Including your own kids. You knew what you were doing persuading me to do that time for your bitch ass. Do you really and truly give a fuck about your kids? Because I guaran-damn-tee if you did, you wouldn't have been out here doing fuck shit to the ones that had your back regardless. Lil bitch ass plan back fired tho." I laughed evilly, pissing him off more as sweat beads lined up on his black ass forehead.

"You killed yo homie Wolf because he knew you and your lil raggedy ass bitch secret. Well, one of y'all secrets out of many. You put a fucking dusty pussy ass hoe before your own flesh and blood. What, you thought killing yo' lil homie was gonna bury your secrets of lies and deceit, huh?" I cracked up laughing and cut his ass off when I saw him trying to open his mouth to defend himself.

"You ain't do shit but open up the can to all the fuck shit you've been doing your whole life. You acted like you didn't fuck with Pops like that because of the shady shit he did but nigga, you are your father's son!" I barked, gritting my teeth. "Usually when a motherfucker talks down on another motherfucker it's because they're just alike! At least the shit Pops did wasn't a secret."

"Yo' Leek. You tripping for real, I'm out this bitch. Holla at me when you get off your fucking rag, homie. You must be bleeding like a lil bitch or something." He stood and made his way to the door.

I trailed his ass, pulling Nina from my waist and placing it to the back of his skull. He was quick and tried to reach for his heat, but I was quicker than his ass. Snatching the gun from his shaky hands, I drew both pistols to the back of his head, one on each side and exhaled. I was about to make the hardest decision in my life, but it needed to be done.

"I really love the shit out my nieces and nephew and don't want any child growing up without a father, but we both know they'll be better off without your bitch ass."

"Really, Leek? I'm your fucking brother, man. Let's talk this shit out, don't do this homie!" He pleaded.

"Yeah, you are my brother, my only sibling. But I have to do this so me and ma can sleep better at night knowing your fool ass ain't out in the world making dumb ass decisions that we have to pay for. You won't send my mother to an early grave behind your back ass bullshit. Everyone is better off without you. Life don't need you here no more, blood. You're a disgrace to the hood, this family and especially those babies. I'll make sure they're taken care of. Now say night night nigga."

I planted two into his dome and walked off feeling relieved as fuck. This was something that was overdue and needed to be done. I would have to repent another day, but at this moment, I felt great as fuck! Don't get me wrong, I loved my big bro with every ounce of my heart, and that's the same reason I had to end that nigga and his foolish games. I wasn't perfect and did my share of fucked up shit too. But never have I ever went against the grain of my family for another motherfucker. J was a disgrace to our hood. I never wanted this to be the way we ended. I gave that nigga the benefit of the doubt, and he still betrayed everything I stood for. He wasn't going to stop. It would've just been a matter of time before he got himself caught up in some more shit. He was just that careless.

I signed for his time with no hesitation and did them years on my dick head. The least he could've done was come clean about that grimy ass bitch instead of keeping her around to continue to crumble what we've built and have her disrespectful ass smiling in my Mama's face. I would've respected him more. He couldn't even be man enough to come clean. He left me in the dark. His own fucking brother.

"Ay yo', Estaban, get the crew to clean this shit up. I'm headed home to my baby," I called over my shoulder and made my way out the warehouse doors.

I jigged to my ride, backing out and dialing my baby's number as I hit the freeway.

"Hey, baby. What time are you coming home?"

"I'm on my way now, bae. What's in them pots. A nigga hungry than a motherfucker!"

"Oh really? I got something for you to eat," Miki cooed, making my dick rise for the occasion.

"For real, boo? What you got for daddy?"

"Some barbecue chicken wings, mac and cheese and greens!" Keke shouted in the background.

"I'mma eat that too and yo' thick ass. Did Mama make it there yet, baby?"

"Yeah, her and Black just pulled up, so hurry home because we're ready to grub."

"A'ight baby. I'll be there soon. I love you."

"I love you too, Malik."

THE END…

Talk to me!

Hey, my Lovies let's discuss these crazy H-Town fools!

Feel free to email me at msgradmarie@gmail.com with your responses....

Who was your most favorite character?

Who was your least favorite character?

How did you feel after Monika's truths started to unravel?

Do you think Malik was wrong for causing his brothers demise?

How do you feel about the Miki & Xavier situation?

Who would you like to see more of?

Again, thanks for reading and don't forget to tell a book Lova to tell a book Lova! Be blessed my loves!

Please be sure to leave a review! And if you enjoyed the *Hooked on a Fifth Ward Menace* series be sure to tell another book lova!

Connect with *Ms. Grad Marie!*

Facebook Author page: https://bit.ly/2HxtOCd

Instagram:

MSGRADMARIE

Are you an avid reader who is interested in joining a readers' group to participate in discussions, contests, giveaways, and view sneak peeks of upcoming releases?

Join Ms. Grad Marie's reading group on Facebook!!

Ms. Grad Marie's Lovies! https://bit.ly/2FdAcuV

Authoress Ms. Grad Marie's Catalog

Share my World with a Savage Like You 1&2 **Complete Series

Stealing the Heart of a Dirty South Hustla' 1-3 **Complete Series

Diary of a Single Mother, Stand Alone Novel

Love Heist : He robbed my heart, Novella

A Thin Line Between Baby Mama And B*tch!

Ash & Omar Forever Loving A Dirty South Hustla', Stand Alone Novel

Hooked on a Fifth Ward Menace 1& 2 **Complete Series

CPSIA information can be obtained
at www.ICGtesting.com
Printed in the USA
LVHW031727101219
640063LV00014B/1117/P